ballad of
the black and
blue mind

ballad of
the black and
blue mind

a novel

anne roiphe

SEVEN STORIES PRESS
new york ◆ *oakland*

Seven Stories Press
140 Watts Street
New York, NY 10013
www.sevenstories.com

College professors may order examination copies of Seven Stories Press titles for free. To order, visit http://www.sevenstories.com/textbook or send a fax on school letterhead to (212) 226-1411.

Library of Congress Cataloging-in-Publication Data

Roiphe, Anne Richardson, 1935-
  Ballad of the black and blue mind : a novel / Anne Roiphe. -- A Seven Stories Press First Edition.
      pages ; cm
    ISBN 978-1-60980-608-8 (hardback)
  1. Women psychiatrists--Fiction. 2. Psychological fiction. I. Title.
  PS3568.O53B35 2015
  813'.54--dc23
                                          2014045875

Printed in the United States

9 8 7 6 5 4 3 2 1

ballad of
the black and
blue mind

one

Dr. H. and Dr. Z. were leaving a meeting of the psycho-analytic journal held at a colleague's house. They each had emptied a few glasses of a good Cabernet Sauvignon, and Dr. Z. had devoured the Saint André cheese, leaving only the yellow rind on the plate and a few broken crackers behind. Because they were cautious men and more aware of the consequences of even the most casual conversation than others who had not made their particular professional choices, they spoke to each other in low voices about Dr. B.

I don't think she recognized me, said Dr. H.

Her comments were strange, said Dr. Z.

She's still the editor-in-chief, said Dr. H.

It's a farce, these meetings, said Dr. Z.

You want to tell her to step down? asked Dr. H.

She would never, said Dr. Z.

She was my supervisor, said Dr. H.

How was she? asked Dr. Z.

A good enough mother to my psychoanalytic self, said Dr. H.

Just that, said Dr. Z.

Just that, said Dr. H.

Can you talk to her? asked Dr. Z.

I can't, said Dr. H.

Years ago I thought about sending my daughter to her, said Dr. Z.

Yes, said Dr. H.

Ronit wasn't interested, said Dr. Z.

Your daughter is an oncologist, isn't she? said Dr. H.

Yes, said Dr. Z.

Dr. Estelle Berman had a new patient. She was the daughter of a colleague, Dr. Herbert Gordon. He was a follower of a branch of psychoanalysis that had challenged some of the older Freudian concepts and gained a considerable following. Dr. Berman had congratulated him on the paper he had given at a conference in Madrid the summer before and as a result he had sent her his daughter, a movie star: a real movie star. When she opened the door Dr. Berman saw with an excited beat of her heart the beauty that had walked past her and taken the patient's seat politely, like a good child. The movie star, two movies, one a critical and financial disaster, was wearing blue jeans with high leather boots and a shirt that showed all that it could and still remain on the body.

The movie star said, Shrinks' kids, we're all crazy, right?

Dr. Berman always found that sentiment irritating. She heard the hostility in the remark: if you're so smart how come your kids are just like everyone else's. As if immunity from life should have been accorded the children of psychoanalysts.

The remark stung. It stung because it was true, there was no good defense, even the best of physicians could not protect their own children from the predators of body and mind that lay outside their homes or dwelled inside their homes. It was true, shrinks' kids went down the drain, just as often as the rest but their parents had begun an inquiry, one still at a primitive stage, but a start, a brilliant start, to our understanding of ourselves, our envies, our lusts, our rage, our love, our tenderness, our small sparks of happiness, our ways of hurting ourselves and others. Is an orthopedist's child not allowed to limp? She did not say this to the girl in her office.

From a certain perspective, Dr. Berman's perspective, no one was normal. Nothing was normal. The human brain vibrated like the universe itself with too many parts to be classified in categories of normal or not. Afflictions were everywhere and so was the glory of the thing, the bravery of loving or hating or wishing or failing. There was a lot of normal failing, that Dr. Berman did admit.

Justine, Betty on her birth certificate, took a pack of Marlboros out of her bag. She was not afraid of death, she announced. Dr. Berman hated the smell of burning tobacco and despised the spill of ashes over her carpet but she knew some patients needed it if they were to talk to her and so she said nothing. Betty, a.k.a. Justine, had the white blonde hair of a Swedish child and the black eyes of a Dostoevsky heroine and those eyes blinked at Dr. Berman nervously. I don't do drugs, she said as if in answer to an accusation. I'll bet, thought Dr. Berman. At least, the patient said, not so much as I used to. Are you making a movie in New York? asked Dr. Berman. She preferred a little small talk to a confrontation on drugs one minute into the first meeting.

No, said Justine. I'm here because my boyfriend is making a movie here. Dr. Berman was clearly supposed to know who the boyfriend was and what movie he was making but she didn't. She was silent. Was being so beautiful a burden? wondered Dr. Berman. Perhaps Justine didn't think she was lovely. Most likely only her face was lovely and her mind ugly as a nest of poisonous ants.

Justine told her story all the while crossing and uncrossing her long legs, smoothing her hair and then tangling it in the next gesture. The tale was about the boyfriend who had left her for a stripper, or almost a stripper, but didn't want the papers to hear of it until the movie he was working on was released and so had forced her to lie to her publicist and everyone which had made her want to steal something which would get her in trouble again. Dr. Berman had missed the news about her arrest in LA over just a small misunderstanding, something she would have fixed if the police weren't after her because they hated her. Rehab was out of the question. Justine would never go into rehab.

Altogether Justine was like a cat in a tree, hissing and showing its claws because it was stuck, up so high and with no way to get down.

Dr. Berman was not afraid of Justine. By the time the forty-five minutes were up, Dr. Berman didn't even think Justine such a great beauty. She saw the tired drawn lines on her face and she saw the nails chewed to the tips, painted with blue glitter and all. She saw the girl's eye makeup run down her cheeks when she admitted to an abortion this boyfriend had demanded. Dr. Berman saw a girl who probably hadn't changed her underwear in days. Her neck wasn't clean either.

Don't steal anything before our next appointment, said Dr. Berman as she stood up, letting Justine know her time was up. Justine smiled and said she would try not to.

She had her fingers crossed.

Stardom, had that become the American dream? Was it the riches or the adulation that followed that made the star an object of worship and envy? Stardom eluded people who were quite able to be themselves, their usual selves. It was not the expectation of those who could feel alive without others' eyes on their private parts. It was for fragile, hungry types, who were looking for themselves in the applause of an audience and that applause always died down.

What was it Justine said she had stolen? It was a fox fur coat because she really didn't approve of buying one, which would support the killing of innocent animals.

Dr. Berman had a bad headache.

Narcissism, what a nasty word, with its professional ring and its cutting finality. It was the obvious word to describe Justine. But what exactly did that mean? Was Justine trapped inside a dank prison of self, a beautiful body, Dr. Berman acknowledged, even if worn at the edges? Was Justine to be envied or pitied? And if the thousands of screaming fans who had almost mobbed her when she went to a nightclub with her boyfriend who was not her boyfriend but was just acting like her boyfriend, knew how deeply Justine wanted someone to keep her in one piece, save her from punishments of her own devising, would they still scream in joy when she traipsed past them on her five-inch heels, steadying herself on the arm of the boyfriend who wished she were someone else?

A girl like this might come from an orphanage, from a series of foster homes in which neglect was not so benign. But this one came from an analyst's home, she had gone to the Lab school in Chicago and had play dates with children whose parents wrote for *The New York Review of Books*. There was something southern in her accent, a Kentucky mountain echo, which she must have learned from music videos since her father had arrived here in his teens from Liverpool and her mother was a violinist from Haifa.

So Justine was a construct made of cameras and the Cloud. Could Dr. Berman turn her into a real girl? Were psychoanalysts, like Geppetto, set up for betrayal by bad little puppets? Why was Justine not real? Justine herself had no interest in the why. It was her father's question and she didn't like it and had no intention of seeking an answer. What she wanted from Dr. Berman was asylum: a safe room where she could hide. Dr. Berman was willing to offer that too. But she also wanted to know why.

On Central Park West, children were stepping off the yellow school buses that rode like migrating elephants down the avenue in the fading light of day. Taxis raced on both sides of the street, passengers coming and going, from their analytic appointments perhaps. Dogs and dog walkers roamed on the other side of the stone fence, along the paths' lines of gray cement benches stretched beneath winter trees, reminders of a wilderness long banished and not mourned. Nearby a playground waited, empty, with swings on rusty chains and a sandbox with an abandoned coffee container on its rim.

Six stories above Dr. Estelle Berman watched as her last patient balanced her coat and bag on one arm and vanished out the door. She sat in the deep leather chair while her shadow lay across the Persian rug she had purchased years ago when she had been a young analyst still in training, attending classes at night, in analysis herself with one of the major figures in her institute, a man who had not expressed openly his admiration for her, his young analysand, but who had, she was quite sure, deep and essential feelings of attraction and longing for her, feelings of course he could not act on, and would not act on, because of the ethics of the profession, because of his esteemed position in the analytic community.

Her apartment had four bedrooms and a maid's room. It had a kitchen with windows that overlooked the yards of the brownstones on the street behind. In the spring the voices of children playing rose to the sixth floor and the rhododendron and pachysandra bushes bloomed.

The apartment:

A long dining room with an oak table that sat twelve.

A living room: wide enough for three couches, two armchairs, two inlaid coffee tables from India, a cabinet of fine Spode, and two rugs from China with dragon tails marking the corners.

Windows looking out over the park.

When it snowed the gentle ridges of earth were marked in dark stripes as the tracks of sleds and skis crisscrossed the white expanse outside the window. In the evening the lamplights glowed and downtown the windows of tall buildings, banks and hotels, offices and stores, illuminated the night sky through which patrolling helicopters on terrorist alert rode uptown to the George Washington Bridge and back over the Statue of Liberty on their nightly route. Higher in the sky, across the park, the white and blue lights of incoming and outgoing planes, fireflies of the industrial world, flickered against the rising moon.

Dr. Berman's office: off the front hall—a large desk with lion paw feet.

The desk: covered with journals and papers and notes and a phone that was never answered during sessions.

On the left a high blue and white Mandarin porcelain vase

filled with fresh cut gladiolas or lilies, or in season, branches of lilacs or forsythia.

A couch on one side of the wall with an afghan blanket folded at its foot.

A beige upholstered patient chair with blue pillow.

Bookshelves:

A floor-to-ceiling bookcase stood against the wall behind the couch. It held the many volumes of *The Psychoanalytic Study of the Child*, books no one needed anymore since the articles were all online. A press of a finger and each could be recalled from the dark recesses of cyberspace where it waited for attention, hibernating through long nights of neglect.

And on the next shelf, the volumes of Freud, *Civilization and Its Discontents*, *Moses and Monotheism*, *Psychopathology of Everyday Life*, *The Interpretation of Dreams*, *Totem and Taboo*, all in faded blue covers, the twenty-three-volume Strachey edition, the three-volume Jones biography, dust on the rims, books that stood guard over her patients, like stars in the sky, looking down on soldiers waiting in trenches, waiting for dawn to rise when they would rush with terrible fear toward the enemy. Dr. Berman was not a tall woman, just a bit over five feet, and to reach the books on the upper shelves she had to call the super who would stand on a chair and bring down the volume she wanted.

A piece of stone pottery engraved with a reproduction of a raven-headed god from the Israeli museum shop, purchased the year the international meetings were in Tel Aviv. (Afterwards she and Howard along with a small group from her institute went on to Cairo and down the Nile.) And in the far corner a biography of Joan Crawford and one of Gloria Swanson.

This was an apartment that spoke of the last century, grander times, when the great buildings along Central Park West were rising one after another filled with New York's newest money, its most recent arrivals, its most fortunate merchants and their families.

It was a rent-controlled apartment.

Who would not be envious of such an apartment, an apartment with four bedrooms and a maid's room. There was also a house in Southampton with a swimming pool and a tennis court. There Dr. Berman spent August, often welcoming psychoanalysts from other continents who were familiar to one another from papers given at international meetings and published in journals of note.

Dr. Berman closed her eyes. She needed to nap, like a cat, like her cat Lily.

Could she sleep now? Was it time? Should she leave her office or should she stay? Did she have another appointment? Where was her book, the black leather book with the days and the hours marked, with the telephone numbers of patients, with a red ribbon to move forward day after day as if one might wrap time like a present, like the gold watch she received for her sixtieth birthday from Howard, her husband, her second husband, the first one is not worth mentioning. Gone, both husbands. Wrong word: dead that second husband, ashes rising in an updraft as seagulls gathered on the dunes at their beach house where every summer, even when his heart was failing, even when his face was drained of color, he had arranged clambakes and picnics for her colleagues and friends. She could almost feel his hand on her shoulder, his big hand. The dancing, he was a good dancer, had stopped. She had felt safe when he was in the room. The bulk of him, the too much weight in the belly, the kindness of him kept her calm: unless it didn't. Four or was it five times she had threatened to divorce him. He was faithful. She less so.

She traveled without him. He traveled only with her. She was the voice in the whirlwind and he was the willow that bent in the storm. She was admired by a host of students and patients and often invited to introduce brilliant and original minds at annual lectures at the Academy of Medicine. He ordered the car that would pick them up after the theater. He arranged for the plumber to fix the leak in the pipes. He was her consort and she was his queen. She liked diamonds and he liked to buy them for her, which he could because he was president of a company that supplied paper products to doctors' offices, including gowns that opened to the front or the back.

She had learned to live alone, alone with her son and the help in the house. If she did not stumble into a memory, or fall upon an empty moment, she managed well. She moved quickly, briskly, keeping the door to old longings closed as tightly as it could close. She had her private regrets. She was not immune to pain.

What had the patient who had just left talked about? What was that patient's name? It was a woman, she was sure of that. The couch was smooth as always. The small towel on the pillow unwrinkled. The patient must have been sitting in the chair, not lying on the couch.

What had the patient who had just left brought to the session? What had she said to the patient? If she were quiet and still it would come back to her. If she didn't let her mind race forward, but thought of serene moments, of waiting for Howard to finish his dessert, of listening to her favorite aria from *La Traviata* with Howard in the next room watching the ball game, then it would come to her suddenly like the smell of her own body on a hot summer day. She waited. It doesn't matter, she said to herself. She picked up Lily and held her in her lap, stroking the gray and white fur, tapping the place between the ears that made the cat purr with contentment. The cat jumped off her lap and left long hairs on her black skirt. She brushed the hairs away and waited, hoping Lily would soon return.

She said aloud the names of places visited, beaches and hotels: was that where the international conference was held where she gave her first paper or was it the auditorium of her son's school, was it a graduation or was it a memorial service, a memorial for whom?

Dr. Berman had not slept well. At four in the morning an ambulance siren had wailed its demented warning as it raced past her block. She had walked to the window and stared out at the eastern sky. The sun beneath the horizon was pushing its way toward her slowly, too slowly. And all through the night she had dreamed: wallpaper from old rooms she once knew well, lamps that had sat on desks in whose drawers she had once hidden a lover's letter as well as the tax forms from the years before, a dress ripped, a glove without its mate, and always the sound of a ringing alarm clock, in the almost darkness of the city where the glow of the blue, green, red Empire State Building, its needle pointed into God's eye, never disappeared entirely. Again she thought about her mother. Her mother had been dead some fifty years and no longer had any skin on her bones, which Dr. Berman knew well enough.

Five hardback copies of her book, *The Nightmare and Its Vicissitudes*, marched along on the shelf behind her chair. Their electric blue covers demanded attention. Her name on the book's spine was clear as a trumpet call. She unpinned her hair and it slipped down over the collar of her suit jacket. Her hair, white at the mostly hidden roots, was a shade of red, auburn, maybe too orange, too even, too perfect, but commanding as she wished it to be.

Her colleagues liked the word *vicissitude*. Freud had used it. It had always sounded to her like the hiss of a snake. She too liked its dangerous echo. Now she was writing a book on memory or she would write a book on memory. Or maybe she could no longer write a book. Actually for her last book, the one titled *Lust and Longing*, she had hired a ghostwriter. She didn't have the time or the energy to write each word herself. It had become hard to form the sentences, to hold them in her head as she was reaching for the next thought. The ghostwriter was a secret. No one would ever know. She would never tell.

Some nights she dreamt in numbers that floated across her brain as if it were a chalkboard. She saw formulas and equations and measurements and theories. She had been the only girl in some classes. But in those classes she had known joy. When she woke from those dreams she felt confident and refreshed, as if somewhere it had rained on dry ground and new seeds might grow.

Things she remembered:

Her mother, what her mother had died of, but she wouldn't say, not now.

A poem she had memorized in the third grade.

She wouldn't say it now. No need.

The medical school auditorium and the boy who took her back to his room after the liver function lecture and what happened there. She could remember that and the stuffed monkey with the pink cotton tongue perched on his bookshelf, a remnant from his childhood home, a sign of immaturity she should have taken seriously.

The corpse, the body, her body, and her partner's, to slice and name. It was female and the pubic hair was black, and the clitoris had withered so it was impossible to find.

The Waterford china plates she had bought in the roadside antique store in Vermont one autumn when they had gone to a wedding. She remembered whose wedding it was: almost. She remembered the inn where they spent the night, the strawberry jam they had for breakfast and Howard running his fingers over her mouth to remove the crumbs that had gathered in the corners.

And then she remembered the red and orange leaves on the trees. They stopped at a road stand to buy a basket of apples, too many apples, most of them soft and bruised.

The black appointment book, there it was under the paper "Object Loss and the Fetish in Early Childhood" that had been sent to her by a Norwegian analyst she had met in Geneva several summers ago.

She had a son. His name was Gerald. She believed in the good enough mother, and all that entailed. But she also believed in spine, upright spine and discipline and order, and she believed that the world rewarded effort. She hired a nanny from Jamaica and went back to work, ten days after Gerald's arrival. She did not alter her teaching schedule. She added patients as referrals came from the head of this committee or that. She became a training analyst the year Gerald started nursery school.

She was interested in sexual obsessions and wrote and delivered papers at meetings across the country and abroad on transsexual identifications and sadistic or masochistic fantasies. She knew why she was interested in sexual obsessions.

Those subjects have many vicissitudes.

If Gerald was not always in her mind it didn't mean that he wasn't present on occasion.

Gerald became a handsome child. She kept his hair long, with bangs hanging almost into his pale blue eyes, and his oblong face, while not like her father's which had been sharp, intense, alert to danger, seemed kind and peaceable. The nursery school report said he was a good sharer and liked to build towers and would try hard to do puzzles if asked. He was pleased when it was his time to water the plants or feed the hamster.

Howard took the boy to the zoo on Sunday mornings when they were in the city and sometimes took him to the office, letting him crayon on printing paper at his assistant's desk. The boy was partial to his father: male identification, a defense against Oedipal feelings. She understood: a normal affliction of early childhood that causes havoc in the brain, until death erases its last trace.

She had read all of Margaret Mahler on separation anxiety and the development of the self in the second year of life. She had read all of Anna Freud's descriptions of the stages of childhood. She knew that sexual thoughts were as natural to the child under seven as the sky above and the soil below. She knew that toilet training involved a separation from what the child misconstrued as a body part, and so became frightened by the flush and disappearance of his own product. She knew that when Gerald woke at night with a dream of fiery dragons about to eat him, or screamed that a building collapse was about to suck him underground, he was only struggling with his desire for her, an illicit desire he would have to abandon.

She read the words of Melanie Klein who was convinced that children wanted to chop up, devour, eat, trample the inner organs of their parents, because of the frustration of their baby genital desires. Maybe or maybe not. She did agree with some of what she had read: underneath the sweetness of the blue pajamas with the little rabbit hopping repeatedly over the sleeves, her son was also in a trap that would not spring. Iron bands of want and need, fastened by fear of retaliation, oiled by guilt, enforced by a desire to murder, accompanied his quite banal childhood. He warmed his little arteries beside a bonfire of ardor for the very persons he might destroy if he weren't so small and so cute in his bunny pajamas.

Sometimes Dr. Estelle Berman looked at Gerald and saw a demon and sometimes she saw a sleepy child whose thumb was often in his mouth, bending his teeth outward, consoling him for the condition of childhood, which would not be altered by any special pleading in any particular instance.

She had a nine-year analysis of her own. Was it successful? Of course it was successful. She had found the root of her ambition and she had recognized that she was flawed. She knew why she was flawed. She forgave herself, or tried to, for the meanness that swelled up within her when she saw a woman more beautiful, more seductive than she. She understood that rivalry was a normal human condition, as common as heartburn and the occasional bad cold. And there was more, much more, she lost her fear of strangers stalking her. She stopped gaining and losing weight with each shift of her mood. She learned to feel almost comfortable in other people's homes, even if they were more expensive and glorious than her own. She learned to listen to other people's boasts and see underneath the bravado, observe the anxiety that settled on the coffee cups after desert. She knew she was a tough lady, and she didn't expect to become a delicate princess.

She had married well in the Victorian novel sense of the word and this gave her insurance against the vicissitudes of life. She had gold pins and thick bracelets set with rare stones. She had necklaces with pearls and real coral. She had gold earrings she caressed with her fingers when she was deep in thought. Her jewelry was not timid or discreet. It admitted to its expense and required respect.

After her own analysis she no longer believed she was a bad person. Or rather she believed that all persons were bad and she, no worse than her neighbor or her friend or her colleague.

Her patients, on the couch or in the chair, accepted her words, gratefully, most of the time. She knew when to speak and when to wait. It was a skill that was perfected with time. She heard the skipped heartbeats, the gasps, the tiny sounds of pain that patients uttered, one and all, as they repeated the tales of their lives, the crucial facts, the losses, avoidable and unavoidable. She responded to the patient or she did not according to some instinct that told her to wait, more is coming, or speak now or the moment will pass and never return. Each session was a dance, a *danse macabre*, not a ball. She was responsible. She was sometimes loved and sometimes hated by her patients. She was almost never bored. Patients lied to themselves, they hid their bitter sharp thoughts, or they spilled them out before her like so many pennies in the blind man's cup, or they wept when they remembered lost love and denied lust. They wept when they saw that their pride was false or their hope futile.

Was she kind? You did not need to be kind to do the work. Was she always right in the way she saw the patient, the story before her, the dream that had been brought to her office? Of course not. She was sometimes right and sometimes kind and frequently she could follow the dream down the royal road of the unconscious and find the buried message that waited there.

Between patients she often changed clothes. She had suits and jackets and shoes for all occasions. She went to professional meetings at her institute. The first Tuesday of every month, she had a committee meeting to discuss the teaching program, the admissions of new students, the appointing of new training analysts. She swam in the waters with others who also knew whom to court, whom to deny, whom to woo. She enjoyed the encounters around the table, in the halls, just as the capos in the back rooms enjoyed their colleagues, their poker games, the urgency of their encounters. She was also an editor of a prominent international psychoanalytic journal which required her to attend meetings in Portugal, in Brazil, in the Loire Valley and other places where psychoanalysts gathered in the summer months, their spouses in tow, their passports in the hotel safe, their afternoons spent in museums and gardens and churches across the globe.

Her father was shot in a bar in Las Vegas over an unpaid gambling debt.

No, that wasn't true, although she often told the story.

He died in a hospital in Charlottesville of cirrhosis of the liver, which was no surprise to anyone, least of all his daughter.

Most of the time, her patients accepted her words gratefully.

Suddenly on a spring day when the dogwood trees in Central Park were just opening their blossoms, a soft white haze on their limbs, Howard Berman felt a deep pain in his chest and within seconds his lips had turned blue and he was gone. He left his wife enough funds to take care of herself and her near-grown son. At the funeral many prominent psychoanalysts wrote their names in the guest book. Some patients of Dr. Berman also appeared and sat in the back of the room. Was her heart breaking? It was hard to tell as she greeted mourners in her living room. She was composed as she had always been. She knew that death was never a surprise, only relatively sudden. It was always there, ignored or not, it was there. She had her ways of keeping together, allowing fear and grief just so much of its due and no more. She was strong, her friends said. Three days after the funeral she resumed her regular schedule and if she was in some kind of pain, makeup hid the traces.

Nevertheless she was mourning. She paced the apartment. She ached in her bones. She came down with a strep infection and when the fever abated she tripped on a rug in her office and fell, spraining an ankle. She was angry too, bristling at the household help, scowling at the doorman, and cutting her friends off in mid-sentence. At night she curled herself into a fetal position and rocked back and forth in her bed. She knew the worst would pass but that was of no comfort as waves of anxiety, how could she continue, washed over her again and again.

She went to a meeting of psychoanalysts, an editorial meeting of a major journal, and she said nothing at all. As the meeting broke up three other analysts, colleagues, asked her to join them in a taxi. They dropped her off at her corner and then watched as she walked in the wrong direction away from her door. One of the doctors jumped out of the cab and grabbed her elbow. This way, Dr. Berman, he said, and walked her through the lobby and right to the elevator that would take her to her apartment. There was talk. She didn't hear it.

In the middle of the night Dr. Berman woke up in her bed, felt about for Howard's arms and legs and his back that was wide and warm with a large mole between the shoulder blades, and remembered that he was gone, and turned on the light. The thought that came to her was not pleasant. She wanted a daughter, a beautiful daughter, whom she would have loved and brought to adulthood. There would be no excess of self-love in her child because she would have been loved enough.

Maybe, maybe not. Dr. Berman knew that like her Chicago colleague, she might have failed. Careful, she warned herself, do not love Justine as if she were yours. Love her only as your patient, which means warily, conditionally, alertly. Wounded birds have a way of dying and sometimes they spread disease.

Lily the cat jumped on the bed, lightly as if a feather had blown onto the blanket.

Justine came late to appointments. The doormen had recognized her and whispered to each other and called down to the superintendent when she came so he could wait in the lobby and catch a glimpse of her long legs when she left. Justine brought her new puppy to her session. It was a small black pug. A gift from an admirer. The pug sat calmly on Justine's lap. Lily jumped down from the windowsill and arched her back and showed her claws and let out a sound between a scream and a choke. The pug opened its sleepy eyes and jumped down and immediately wet the carpet. Was that the point, to stain something that belonged to her doctor? Dr. Berman picked up Lily and tossed her into the hall. She would have liked to do the same to Justine. But she said instead, Tell me about the abortion, and Justine with more drama than necessary described it all. There was no surprise there for Dr. Berman.

Justine didn't show up for her next appointment or the one after that.

Dr. Berman walked in the park and considered what mistake she might have made. How could she hold this movie star who always got what she wanted and never got what she wanted? What would have happened if she had let Lily scratch the eyes out of that pug?

She called Justine, just to remind her of her next appointment. I'd like to see you, she said, even if that was not as professional as it ought to have been.

Justine returned. The boyfriend left for Italy for a vacation with his new love. Justine did not want a new love. She wanted to sleep all day and watch television until the stations turned dark.

One of her security staff took the puppy for his children who lived in Long Beach in a small house not far from the ocean.

Justine did not need or want antidepressants. She had her own medicine cabinet and her ways of restocking it whenever necessary.

Dr. Berman answered her phone when it rang loudly at two in the morning. It was Justine wanting to tell her some childhood memory, a sexual play with a neighbor boy. Justine wanted to have all of Dr. Berman, all her waking hours and her sleeping ones as well. Dr. Berman told Justine that she would see her at her appointment later in the week. Her voice was neutral, her tone warm enough, but the truth was Dr. Berman did not like being called in the middle of the night. If she had she might have been an obstetrician.

Justine told Dr. Berman about her mother's boyfriend who was supposedly painting her mother's portrait but then it appeared as if he had more in mind than a nude descending a staircase. Justine had been brought to his studio one afternoon and the painter had put his fingers in her vagina when her mother was fixing tea in the kitchen down the hall.

Justine's mother did not believe her. Justine's mother often said things to her father in a language that Justine couldn't understand. Neither of course could her father but that didn't appease Justine. Also, this mother insisted on sending Justine to a kibbutz where she had to clean out cow dung. Three summers lost, said Justine.

I hate her, Justine said.

We'll see, said Dr. Berman.

No, said Justine, I really hate her.

Yes, said Dr. Berman.

Do you think I'm beautiful? asked Justine one day.

Do you think you're beautiful? Dr. Berman returned the question.

Everyone thinks I'm beautiful, said Justine.

And you? asked Dr. Berman.

Justine didn't like the question and she didn't answer it.

Some months later Justine said something that pleased Dr. Berman, enough for a real smile.

She said, I think you should call me Betty. I'd like that.

Dr. Berman said, Betty is a good name.

Justine had already tried to drown Justine in a river of vodka.

Then one Thursday morning when the penguins in the zoo were diving into their pool, behind the glass wall that separated them from the visitors who admired the penguins because they endured their imprisonment in the stage set that had become their home without visible signs of misery, Justine, who walked through the park on her way to Dr. Berman's office, followed by her security people, was jostled by a stranger who put his hands on her chest, before the guys could grab him and shove him and chase him away.

I hate this city, she said to Dr. Berman.

And she decided to go back to LA She had heard from her former boyfriend who was now over the stripper, who was actually an up-and-coming actress who was on location in India, and he had asked Justine to return to him. If she didn't come right away, he might kill himself.

Really? asked Dr. Berman.

Maybe, said Justine.

At their last session, Justine brought a present for Dr. Berman. I might be back, she said.

After she left Dr. Berman opened the gift. She found a necklace, emerald and diamonds and a large black pearl at the center in a Duane Reade tissue box. In the box was a note in tiny handwriting. *This came from Cartier's. You can't return it. Don't mention my name if anyone asks where it came from. Thanks and love from Betty.*

Daughters grow up and leave, thought Dr. Berman. Even real daughters do that. Patients interrupt their treatment before they are ready to be on their own and psychoanalysts lose their patients before they are ready to let them go. It happens all the time. Dr. Berman could tell you about others, other times. But that night she opened a good bottle of Merlot that Howard had been saving for her birthday, the one he missed by dying, was it five years ago or more? She stood at her window and watched the people in their warm winter coats walking dogs, rushing along to the theater, to dinner at the restaurant a few blocks away, to a wedding perhaps, or a celebration of a promotion or a victory of some kind over someone else of course. She saw the lights in the apartments across the park, small flickers in the distance, where people were gathered, families were building up resentments in the way that families do, envy and fear served with the evening's microwaved lamb chops.

Standing at the window like one of those figureheads at the prow of a sailing ship, a figure carved in wood, painted reds and blues and yellows to show the sea that the ship was protected by a large and looming female. She felt wooden, as if her limbs would not bend on command. She felt cold and useless.

If she had a real daughter she might call her now. But she did not.

A few nights later she was listening to a paper at a seminar meeting titled "Passive-Aggressive Behavior and Personality Disorders." They were in a meeting room at the institute seated at a round table, small bottles of sparkling water had been placed in front of all the participants, a recording machine on a small trolley glowed red to signal its working state. The presenter was speaking in a low voice. Dr. Berman leaned forward in her seat. She could hardly make out the words. The young woman appeared to be whispering into the microphone. Dr. Berman closed her eyes and fell asleep. All the participants at the seminar including the speaker pretended not to notice. The speaker, who had been a student of Dr. Berman's in her third year at the institute, wondered if she was boring everyone there. A few of the other younger participants thought that the paper was less well done than they had originally thought. But the older analysts understood: the day is long, the effort of listening takes its toll, sometimes even the best of the analyzed are awake in the small hours of the morning and sleepless they flounder through their day.

Sometimes the mind has had enough of other people's words and wants to be alone with itself.

Dr. Z. said to Dr. H., Did you see the necklace Estelle was wearing tonight?

Dr. H. hadn't noticed the necklace because he had a cataract in his left eye and had no interest in women's wear, a fact his wife had complained about often.

Why? he asked Dr. Z.

Dr. Z. said, It looked like diamonds and emeralds and quite extraordinary.

Dr. H. said, Real?

Dr. Z. said, I don't know.

Dr. H. said, Probably not. Who would wear such a thing to a discussion of "Femininity and Fantasy in the Silent Film."

Dr. Z. said, Boring talk.

Dr. H. said, Very.

Dr. Z. said, I'm a Sherlock Holmes fan.

Dr. H. said, Me, I prefer Star Wars.

Dr. Z. said, The boy in you.

Dr. H. said, The boy in me.

Dr. Z. said, I had a patient who told me his favorite moments of every W. C. Fields movie ever made. Also all Marx Brothers and Abbott and Costello plots.

Dr. H. said, How long did that go on?

Dr. Z., Too long.

Dr. H., What was he doing?

Dr. Z., Stalling.

Dr. H., And then?

Dr. Z., He was killed in a car crash.

Dr. H., Not funny.

Dr. Z., No.

two

Anna Fishbein was home. She had arrived several weeks after the start of the second semester. She had brought with her two suitcases, a duffel bag of laundry, her bear that had shared her childhood bed, a book of Sylvia Plath poems that she always carried in her backpack, and a glazed look in her eyes. Her mother was afraid it was drugs. Her father was afraid it was alcohol. Anna glared at her parents. They had no faith in her. She was not using drugs and she was not drinking, no more than her dorm mates at least. She had come home, she said, to stay. That was all she would say.

Anna's mother, Beth, was on the faculty at St. John's University. She had published two well-regarded books on Virginia Woolf. Her father, Fritz, was a biographer. His interest was American history, the Civil War in particular. His own father had escaped from Vienna and his mother had spent her early childhood in a small town in Cuba, where in an unlikely migration many Yiddish speakers had washed ashore. But it was the Civil War that held his attention. When asked by interviewers, TV anchors, or such why he had chosen this subject, he said, "If history were an MRI, the Civil War would be revealed as the site of the tumor, the place where the shadows extended outward promising a painful future." He had said this often.

History did not interest Anna. It was hard enough to understand the present, the moment that was disappearing even as you began to see its shape.

You need to do something, said Beth to her daughter. Yes, said Anna. Do you want to do some research for me? asked Fritz. I'll pay you, he added. Anna did not respond. Anna took to sleeping almost until noon. She took the dog for long walks. She washed her hair again and again. This is not all right, said Beth. Fritz said, This is not normal. This is not just a stage. Anna's brother Meyer was studying for his PSATs. He complained that Anna stole money from him. Beth left a few hundred dollars on Anna's bureau.

Beth and Fritz went out to their favorite Chinese restaurant and all they could talk about was Anna. What? What? How? they asked each other. They liked each other less because of Anna. On the other hand they could barely be apart, because no one else understood their shorthand, their anxious return to the same words again and again. What, what? How?

Which is how Anna, referred by a college friend of Beth's who was a psychoanalyst, came to Dr. Berman's office, on a Thursday morning, on a cold February day, bored, indifferent, with a high wall surrounding her and a very strong conviction that her life would be short and uneventful.

She was wearing a sweatshirt, jeans, and her long hair curled freely down her back, an invitation not echoed in her eyes.

Tell me, Anna, said Dr. Berman in a voice that promised not to judge, only to listen. Tell me what makes you happy. I'm not happy, said Anna. Of course, said Dr. Berman, but even so something makes you happy. Anna said nothing. She looked out the window and saw the bare trees in the park and said nothing. Dr. Berman waited. Anna waited. Anna said I'm happy enough. Good, said Dr. Berman, then let's talk about what makes you unhappy. Nothing, said Anna, but a few tears appeared at the edges of her eyes and her nose turned red. We can talk about that nothing, said Dr. Berman. Maybe, said Anna, and she looked down into her lap so that the doctor would not see the flicker of hope that like a sparrow in flight had passed over her face and disappeared as quickly as it came.

We can consider some medication, said Dr. Berman. That might make you feel better. Drugs, said Anna, are you pushing narcotics? Dr. Berman smiled. This was a sign of life. If you need them, we can consider it, she said. No, said Anna, I don't do drugs. How about medicine? said Dr. Berman. Do you use antibiotics? Anna said nothing. We'll see, said Dr. Berman. Anna said nothing. Dr. Berman's use of the *we* pleased Anna in a small way.

Dr. Berman had gone through a checklist in her mind, drugs, maybe, anorexia, no. The girl seemed about ten pounds overweight. Depression, of course, but in what particular way? Separation issues, yes, but what else? Fury, maybe, but fury was like a shadow, everyone has it in the right light. Was she bright enough? Hard to tell. Was there something in there waiting to reveal itself, a talent, a capacity, a sweetness unexpected by those who knew her best, maybe? On the other hand she might be just another girl struggling with some sexual urge, unacceptable to her, uninteresting to Dr. Berman. Dr. Berman believed that it was a miracle that the impulses that beset the human mind did not break out and cause havoc more often, holy murder, in the bedrooms, boardrooms, streets.

Anna did agree to see Dr. Berman three times a week, Monday, Wednesday, Friday at 11:15. She had nothing else to do.

Anna texted her best friend from high school. Home, she said. Deciding what to do next. That night Anna listened to her music on her iPod, watched a vampire movie on late night TV, washed her hair, told her brother no girl would ever be interested in him. Just as sleep seemed to be possible, her body shook with some inner alarm and she was wide awake again, and she went into the bathroom and from her makeup kit removed a razor. She opened the razor and carefully between thumb and forefinger took out the blade. She sat on the edge of the bathtub and gently, tentatively, ran the blade over her arm below the elbow. And then to the side of the vein, careful to avoid the vein, she pressed the blade down into her skin and she felt the sharp bite. She watched as a spill of blood oozed over her flesh. It fell in a splotch on the tub rim and then slid crimson and beautiful down the white porcelain.

And then she went back to bed and fell asleep. Her bear had fallen to the floor.

She shouldn't sleep all day, said her father as he drank his morning coffee in the kitchen. I know, said her mother. I'll wake her, said her father. I don't know, said her mother, maybe she was up late last night.

Beth wanted a cigarette. Her last cigarette was eight years ago. Once in a while the need came on her, like a hunger pang. It could be ignored. She ignored it. Fritz looked pale. His left eye blinked too rapidly. He was a tall man but now when he stood up there was something of the scarecrow about him, a kind of inner collapse. The cells of his body were losing their shape, their self-respect. You should wake her, he said to his wife. She didn't rise from her chair. You wake her, said Beth in her fake voice, the one she used for salespeople and doormen. Fritz flinched. He noticed a pale wart that had sprung up on her neck.

The seven-room apartment on West End Avenue that the Fishbein family had bought with the funds received when Fritz's father had died was in need of painting, the Persian carpet in the study had lost its deep purple hues and the couch had a rip in the leather that Beth had patched with tape and now gave the room the appearance of a drunk who had been in a fight the night before, with someone unremembered over something not so urgent in the light of day. The disrepair was not caused by financial concerns. It was hard enough to find time to read the periodicals, the political journals, the manuscripts and theses proposals that piled up in abandoned chairs, on coffee tables, stacked in the corners of the bedroom, on dresser tops. No time at all for the superficial, the surface of style. Or was the leather rip a style of its own, a vote for mind over matter? There was a TV in the living room. It was flat as the world in a fourteenth-century map. It came to life for the Sunday talk shows, for CNN, for Yankees games and Sunday football and HBO series. Meyer downloaded science fiction movies on his computer and Anna wouldn't tell her parents what she watched. Probably *Oprah*, said her mother. Porn, said Fritz. Oh God, said her mother, whose paperback copy of *The Story of O* was on a top shelf, high up but within reach and never out of memory.

Only the fearful and the pretentious avoided TV, Fritz said, a real swimmer dives into all waters, deep, shallow, salt, fresh, narrow, wide.

Was there an unhappy love affair? Fritz asked his wife. Daughters might tell their mothers something like that, something ordinary that would pass over, leaving them all unharmed, the way they had been once upon a time. I don't know, said Beth, she hardly speaks to me. It wasn't always that way. The way it had been, was that an illusion? Once upon a time she would come home from her last class and her daughter would rush to her side. Once she felt free with her child, free of all the effort and the discriminations and the distinctions she made each moment of her working life. She felt only the word *home*, the word *child*, the safety of her armchair, her rose quilt, her daughter's hair that she brushed in the mornings and sometimes braided.

Had they let something slip, something fall down, something they were supposed to do but didn't? Had they harmed, not meaning to, but harmed the person they had created between them, thigh to thigh, heat rising, and with good intentions perfectly aided by the moonlight flooding the cedar planks in the floor of the cabin they had rented by the lake for two weeks in August? Do you remember that summer we went to Maine? asked Fritz. Yes, said Beth, who then opened her black bag and took out a memoir she was preparing for her Thursday seminar, a story of survival in a women's prison. The narrator wrote in brave sentences that bristled, holding the reader the way any car crash would, with fire, crumpled metal, broken glass, a body on the tarmac.

Fritz had an office twenty blocks away. He walked there as he did most weekdays. All the way uptown, he kept the image in his head of his daughter's face, a kind of blankness, making it seem more like a mask than a face. It frightened him, this face of the child he had created, valued, overvalued? Even a confident man, with five significant books listed in the congressional library's catalogue, has days when his faith in himself is shaken.

Dr. Berman looked at Anna sitting across from her in the large patient's chair. Her cat Lily sat on the window ledge asleep.

Felines could not break patient confidentiality. Dr. Berman suppressed a sigh. It was going to be a long forty-five minutes. Anna did not seem pleased to be there. She did not seem comfortable in her chair. She played with the ends of her hair. She looked out the window intently as if she were immensely curious about something happening in the park across the street. Dr. Berman was not going to rush matters but wasn't going to sit in silence either. Did you have a roommate? she asked. Yes, said Anna. Did you have any particular difficulty with her? asked Dr. Berman. No, said Anna. She was all right. Did you find the work hard? asked Dr. Berman. No, said Anna. Dull? asked Dr. Berman. Yes, said Anna. Tell me about your classes, said Dr. Berman. Anna said nothing. Dr. Berman tried another direction. Did you have a boyfriend? No, said Anna. Did you want one? said Dr. Berman. Anna said nothing. Did you want a woman? For what? said Anna. Were you perhaps sexually attracted to women? Dr. Berman's voice was neutral. She might have been asking if Anna preferred Gouda or Brie. Anna said nothing. Have you had intercourse, sex with anyone? she asked. Anna said nothing. Dr. Berman said, Anna, you came home suddenly. You left college, you say you will not return. You cannot hide whatever grieves you here. I need your help in order to help you. I don't need your help, said Anna, but there was a tremble in her voice. Dr. Berman heard it. Yes you do, she said. Her voice was like a whisper, soft but insistent. I have to leave, said Anna. No, said Dr. Berman, it's not time. You seem sad, she said. What is making you sad? Nothing, said Anna, but her eyes filled with tears. I don't know, said Anna. We'll find out, said Dr. Berman. Anna said, I don't care. You care, said Dr. Berman, and then she added, perhaps unwisely, Talk to me. And Anna thought but didn't say, Never. Dr. Berman heard the *never* which might mean *maybe* even though it was silent, the way we know there is an *e* at the end of words like *done* or *whole*, or *mine* or *have*: maybe especially the word *mine*.

The next session she asked Anna what she had thought she would do with her life when she was in high school. Anna said, I wanted to be a war correspondent. I wanted to write about the bodies of the soldiers who were hurt or killed. If you could, asked Dr. Berman, would you do that now? Yes, said Anna. I would. But it might be dangerous, said Dr. Berman. That wouldn't bother me, said Anna. I'm not afraid. But you are afraid to tell me what brought you home, said Dr. Berman. Anna said nothing. At the end of the session when Anna stood up and turned to the door, she said to Dr. Berman, I am not afraid. Good, said Dr. Berman.

Dr. Berman wondered about incest. Anna and that writer father, it was possible. Incest was an interest of hers. She had written three papers on the subject published in the international psychoanalytic journal and she had delivered one of the papers at the meeting in Mexico City the previous July. She had worn her red summer suit with a gold pin in the shape of the sun on the lapel. Nothing human was alien to her, but some things were more compelling than others. She had no doubt that attractions to shoes or nail clippings or animal fur were just signals from the dark, products of the want and disappointment that ran through the mind, everyone's mind. Untamed thoughts, formed in the crucible of rage and need, corrupted by civilization's niceties were common enough. Dr. Berman considered herself a kind of exterminator. She was after the lice of the mind. The putrid stuff within took no holiday, spared no one, lasted to the final breath and only then disappeared. Dr. Berman did not believe in the afterlife or the salvation of the soul. She did like being the chairwoman of psychoanalytic committees that determined matters of importance and affected the lives of others. At the last meeting when the talk turned to narcissistic personality disorders she had mentioned that she knew Justine Fast and while she wasn't explicit about their relationship she did imply some knowledge of Justine's absence from the public eye. She did manage to hint at the difficulty of treatment in such instances but express her confidence that all was well in hand. She shouldn't have done that. She did it. If you treat a famous person and you don't tell anyone you would be a candidate for sainthood and Dr. Berman was not interested in being canonized: simple awe and envy would do.

It was hard to tell if the girl was intelligent. She would have to penetrate the shell and see. Anna would resist. Her therapist would pursue without seeming to pursue. Her therapist would have to be patient, patient but stealthy.

Dr. H. and Dr. Z. were waiting downstairs for Dr. Berman. They were taking her to a dinner party for a visiting psychoanalyst from Zurich, one who had published original work on infant development. She was late. He asked the doorman to call upstairs. She was coming, the doorman said, soon.

Dr. H. asked Dr. Z., Are you afraid of losing your mind?

Dr. Z. said, Of course, isn't everyone?

Dr. H. said, Not those who have already lost their minds.

Lucky at last, said Dr. Z.

Fritz was in his office, idling at his computer, an email to a colleague about a seminar at Texas A&M the following December, an appeal for an urgent contribution from the Democratic Party, a reminder from his editor of a luncheon with booksellers still some months away. He put his hand on his stomach. He rolled it over the excess flesh. He should lose weight. He should take his bike out into the park. He should sleep better. He could feel the ache behind his eyes, a mark of his predawn tossing in sheets. He had tried to wake his wife but she resisted, so far into her own Ambien sleep she had left him stranded in the bed they shared. The radiator in the apartment was turned up too high. The room was hot. It was too cold to open a window. The heat was controlled in the basement. It was like a sauna in that bedroom.

All he had ever wanted was that his children should be happy. Fritz was an honest man: that was not all. He had also expected a certain giftedness, an extraordinary ability in something, music, art, mathematics, scholarship. He had not wanted ordinary children. But then no one wants ordinary children. Fritz understood: if some children were to be extraordinary then most had to be ordinary. For now, all he wanted was Anna talking on the phone to a friend, her lilting voice filled with the sound of light rainfall on the moving river.

Later he listed certain disappointments: Anna gave up the piano and the flute. Anna was not a reader, a real reader, like he had been, like he still was, although she was an A student, he knew she worked hard but learning wasn't as easy or natural for her as it had been for him. Anna was not a chess player. He had tried. Anna was not a dancer. He knew it after the first recital. Anna was not an athlete. She tried out for teams but didn't make them. Anna was dear to him, but not extraordinary. At least she had not yet discovered her gift.

And what if she had no gift? It mattered to him. It didn't matter to him. It shouldn't matter to him, on that point he was clear.

Anna received an email from her roommate. When are you coming back? Never, she wrote in return. She thought about never. *Never* was a beautiful word. There was Peter Pan in Never Never Land. There was a way that never was just like forever. It was a verdict, an end to so many questions. It was better than next, or soon, or eventually. It was firm, solid, definite. Never, she was never going back.

Anna wore a shirt she had taken from her father's drawer. It was a blue shirt, soft with tiny white buttons. She rolled up the sleeves just over her wrists and opened the shirt so that her breasts just peeked out, a shy promise, a diversionary tactic. There were small white scars on her arms. There were newer dark lines. There were thin cuts that still leaked red blood onto the bandages she had tenderly placed there. At night she listened to the music that intruded into her ears through the wires attached to her laptop. She didn't think about the future. She didn't think about her old friends. She didn't consider her old ice skates resting on the closet floor. She floated in the sound as if she were a fall leaf torn from its branch in all the unremarkable ways of leaves and wind and seasons.

Beth was at lunch with an older colleague: her colleague's daughter was pregnant. This would be the first grandchild. It makes me feel old, said the colleague, but the way she said it, the smile that flickered across her face, sent another message. It was like the lighthouse bell ringing off the shore, all is well, all is well. The rocks may be dangerous, the passage to the port uncertain, the winds strong, but no crash has occurred tonight, the moon is out, the waves are calm, calm now, if not tomorrow. A pressure formed in Beth's head. Anna, she wanted to say, was home. She didn't say it. Anna is stranded, she wanted to say, but she didn't. If she said it out loud it would be true. If she didn't say it out loud it would still be true. Also the Vita Sackville-West memoir she was reading had suddenly lost its luster. It seemed manipulative, false. That she could talk about and did.

Fritz considered. Had he been overly seductive with his daughter, had he tried to keep her for himself, such things are possible. He had to ask himself hard questions and answer them bravely. Was his own fear of failure, the one that had been with him ever since he had learned that people fell off high wires and crashed into the dirt and that the best of safety nets ripped and that there was no time of night or day when the smell of blood wasn't in the waters—*Deutschland über alles*? Had his daughter absorbed his fear and made it her own?

Beth, back at her desk in her office, a photo of her two children in a silver frame sitting to the left of her computer, wondered if she should have stayed home, could the Neanderthals who carped at mothers who hired help, mocked those who didn't work at the school fair, who had no time for tea parties in the afternoon, were they right after all? Had she neglected the most important work of her life, for this desk, for this title, for her own selfish needs? Yes, and yes, and yes, she accused herself. But there was a defense: she made the defense. She picked up the phone to make an appointment with Dr. Berman to talk about the situation. Dr. Berman returned her call some hours later and said she couldn't see her. It didn't matter who was paying the bill. She was Anna's doctor. She could recommend someone for Beth. Beth was not interested. Beth was not the kind of woman to let tears fall, certainly not in the office, not with students apt to knock at her door, not at home either, not in front of Fritz who ought to be crying too but probably wasn't. She put the book she was teaching and a batch of student papers in her black bag and left the office early. She would talk to Anna herself.

When she got home she found Anna was out. Anna was siting in the park.

She was smoking. Passersby glared at her as if she didn't know that smoking was dangerous. So what, thought Anna, so, so what?

That evening at dinner Fritz said to his daughter, What is it you want to do? Anna did not look at him. She was stabbing her fork into her peas. Stop that, said Fritz. Anna said nothing. What is the matter with you? he shouted. You have food and clothes, a nice room, parents who love you. The Nazis aren't chasing you. The slave hunters aren't trying to return you to your master. You don't have cancer, or multiple sclerosis. You're not blind or deaf. You have all your limbs. You don't owe vast sums of money. You have not been arrested for any wrongdoing I know about. For God's sake grow up.

Fritz was afraid to look his wife in the eye. She would be appalled at his outburst. But in his chest he could feel relief like a sailor sighting shore. There, he had said it and he was right. He hadn't said she was spoiled and selfish and peculiar. He had edited out those thoughts. He had said enough. Anna took another stab at her peas. The sleeve of her shirt, her father's shirt, slipped into the curry sauce on the shrimps delivered from the Indian restaurant on Columbus Avenue.

Anna jumped up and ran into her room. She took off the shirt and threw it into the hamper in her bathroom and turned around to see her mother entering the door. Her mother saw the cuts on her arm, a lineup of cuts, a few bandages wrapped all the way around the forearm where the cuts had been particularly deep. Her mother quickly closed the door. What she had seen made no sense. Who had hurt Anna?

Once when Anna was in third grade her best friend told her she wasn't her best friend anymore. Anna had refused to eat for two days. But then she made a new friend. Once at camp Anna had called and asked her parents to pick her up. It had something to do with a boy from across the lake who had said her eyes were crossed. They weren't. They told her to call again if she still wanted to come home at the end of the week. She didn't. When at the end of the summer they went to the bus stop in White Plains Anna cried in her counselor's arms because camp was over.

Beth was angry at Fritz. If it was her fault it was his fault. Fritz decided to go to work at his desk. He didn't want to hear his wife breathe. She almost smelled of confusion and disappointment. He couldn't bear the weight of her soul. It was too heavy. It smothered him.

Beth considered: drugs, drugs were the destroyers of children's minds, their sense of purpose, their relationship to their mothers and fathers and brothers and sisters. Drugs were the seducers promising immediate pleasure and guaranteeing loss, loss of clarity, loss of a future. Oh Mr. Tambourine Man, what have you done with my child? But Anna didn't seem to be on drugs. Beth had searched her room, rummaged through old papers, found a list of clothes she had wanted for college.

Had someone rejected her? Who? Was it sexual? Was she struggling with gender identity? Beth would not be shocked. It was a new world. Anna could love anyone she liked as long as she loved. Fritz would agree. Was she afraid she wouldn't do well? She had always done well.

Beth was suddenly afraid to talk to Anna. She didn't want to say the wrong thing. She wanted to help but anything she said might make matters worse. The thought seared her brain: Anna might hate her, must hate her, wouldn't really look at her. Had she delivered a stillborn child who happened to be eighteen years old?

Fritz said, I want to talk to Dr. Berman. Beth said, She doesn't want to talk to us. We pay her, said Fritz. She has to talk to us. Insist, he said. Beth insisted.

Dr. Berman had referred the Fishbeins to Dr. Z. He noticed the half-completed gesture of Fritz who had wanted to hold his wife's hand and then changed his mind. He offered no thoughts speculative or otherwise about Anna. He listened. His phone rang. He ignored it. He asked if the parents were planning a divorce. They weren't. He asked if Meyer was having trouble with friends or schoolwork. He wasn't. He asked if Anna had had an abortion that they knew of. They didn't think so. He assured the parents that many children found their first year away from home difficult. He did not think the problem was unusual. Let's see how it goes, he said. She's in good hands with Dr. Berman. He hoped that was true. Beth wanted to mention the blood on Anna's arms but she thought that might be a betrayal of her daughter. Maybe it was nothing, nothing worth mentioning.

Afterward, as they waited for the elevator and put on their coats, Fritz pinched Beth in the spot above her second rib which was his signal to her, come lie down with me, leave the TV, leave the dishes, leave the children, lie near me, naked, now. Beth pulled away. She did not look at him. In the street as Beth waved down a taxi to take her to the university, Fritz said, Cold fish. Beth sighed. Was he talking about her or Dr. Z.? It would not be so bad, she thought, to be a cold fish, a cold fish with a slice of lemon for an eye.

In the cab she considered, was there a circle in hell for failed mothers? She would have liked to have wept or to have howled, instead she closed her eyes and thought of herself on a beach blanket near the ocean's edge listening to the pounding waves, the hissing of spray, the way the meditation counselor had taught her when she'd had a cluster of migraines after Meyer's birth.

Beth was not sleeping. Fritz was not sleeping. He felt a vague fluttering of unsatisfied desire and turned to his wife. She was lying there stiff, her limbs close to her body, all on her side of the bed. He could sleep if she would come to him. But she didn't want to. She didn't want sex, she wanted happiness and that she could not have. Fritz got up from the bed, put on his robe, and fixed himself a pastrami sandwich with a pickle. He walked to Anna's room and listened for sounds of music or talk. He might go in, he might ask her what is wrong. He might rumple her hair as he did when she was six. He might tell her a story or play his Rolling Stones tapes for her. The light was on, he could see it, pale but inviting, slipping under the crack of the closed door. He knocked. It's me, he said, Can I come in? Go away, she said in the voice of a child. He stood there, uncertain. Go away, she said again. He did. He went to the kitchen and ate his sandwich in the dark. He spilled pickle juice on the table and left it there.

Meyer had a nightmare. In it an alien was oozing through the slats of the air conditioner. He was watching it push through, translucent flesh, claws like icicles and bulbous eyes that fixed on Meyer sitting up in his bed. He woke breathing hard and his hand reached down to his organ. All right. Just a dream. Dreams had meaning, his father had explained. Something to do with forbidden wishes. He did not wish to be eaten by an alien. He rose to go to the window and heard the water running in the bathroom. His sister must be there. He decided to go tell her his dream. He went to the door and would have knocked but it was open a crack already. Anna was sitting on the edge of the bathtub. There was blood. In her hand was a razor. Meyer jumped away from the door. He was still dreaming. He rushed back to his bed and tried to wake up. After a little while he did.

Before she sat down in Dr. Berman's office Anna took off her sweatshirt. She was wearing a tight T-shirt and at first Dr. Berman saw only her small breasts and an outline of the nipples, and then she saw the scars and the fresh cuts and the scabs. She did not immediately remark on the elephant that was now clearly in the room. Ah, one of those, she thought. This would not be a short treatment. This girl before her might be just at the beginning of a long slide down, a slow journey into invalidism, hospital corridors, curiosity in the eyes of her old friends. On the other hand maybe not. Dr. Berman suddenly was tired. Did she have the strength for this? Did she really want to ride this ride into the tunnel with this child? She intended to have her hair done this afternoon after her last appointment. Her red hair held firm like a helmet, but the dull gray roots like repressed memories kept reappearing.

Anna looked at her and waited. Dr. Berman said, Monkeys in cages are known to tear at their fur and pierce their skin and birds in cages can peck at their bodies until they bleed. What kind of a cage are you in? Anna said, I don't watch *Animal Planet*. Dr. Berman said, How long has this been going on? Since the month before I went to college, said Anna. Do you want it to stop? asked Dr. Berman. Yes, said Anna. This wasn't a very convincing yes, it wasn't a heartfelt yes, but it was a yes, nevertheless.

Beth was tired. Did she need a calcium supplement? Beth woke in the morning with a cramp in her leg. On her way to her eleven o'clock class Beth heard her cell phone ring and she was afraid, what now? It was the dry cleaners, they had found her missing gray blouse. There was a certain light that had left her eyes, Fritz noticed. Meyer who never paid any attention to his mother noticed. At dinner he complimented her blue jacket and he asked her if she wanted him to get her anything when he walked the dog. Her cell phone had an icon that glowed a radioactive green to illustrate how much power was left in its storage hold. Her own power she felt had drained below 20 percent and when it was all gone she would go blank. No people chargers existed. Fritz made excuses to stay out late. He was working at his office. He needed to go to Chicago to do some research for a few days.

Beth was like one of those clouds you notice when lying on your back at the beach, at first it has a shape, a donkey, a unicorn, a mountain with a tree on top, and then as the winds move on the shape changes and the cloud breaks up into several blurred pieces and you can't make out any form at all and your eye turns away. The cloud cannot sustain interest once it has come apart.

Would you like to be my research assistant for a few months? Fritz asked his daughter. She was silent. There are some letters in the library that a soldier wrote home to his sister and she saved them. I need to have them available while I'm writing. Anna looked down at her feet. She had no interest in letters from a long gone battlefield. A wave of boredom came over her, a wave so high, so forceful that it might have been a tsunami of boredom. She could drown in her own disinterest. She thought of her razor, its thin blade waiting for the early hours of dawn for her attention. She thought of her knee with the wide white scar from the time she fell on a rock in the park at the sixth-grade field day. She ran her fingers over her scar. I'm busy, she said to her father. Doing what? he asked in a tone that he had not meant to use and embarrassed him as it echoed in the room. Beth said, Leave her alone. Anna cast her mother a thank you look and Fritz seemed fascinated by a report on CNN from a faraway place where some young man had set himself on fire in protest over ever-present tyranny—lack of religious freedom, and an inability to feed his young child. The act disgusted Fritz. He could not take his eyes from the screen as the footage ran over and over again and the flames, starting small at the base of the man's legs, rose higher and brighter. The camera was held in the hand of someone standing on a distant balcony. Fritz could not see the burning man's features.

Anna had left the room. She lay down on her bed. She text messaged her roommate, What's up? NM, came back the answer. A circle had closed, excluding her. She had left and in leaving all conversations had been cut off as if a power surge had disabled her friendships.

Dr. Berman, she said the next Thursday, I have no friends. Did you ever have friends? Dr. Berman asked. I did, Anna said. Then you'll have them again, said Dr. Berman. When? said Anna. When you're ready, said Dr. Berman.

Tell me about your last boyfriend, said Dr. Berman.

I haven't had a boyfriend, said Anna.

No one you hoped would be your boyfriend? said Dr. Berman.

No, said Anna. She was lying.

Beth missed a lunch with the head of her department. Her graduate assistant was out sick and Beth had forgotten to look at her calendar. She spent time picking at the severe wound to her own pride. What was that pride? Had it been overweening, did she tempt the gods to humble her? She didn't believe in gods or God but she had no doubts about humbling. She had felt a condescending rush of pity when her friend Ellen's daughter had been sent to rehab in Minnesota. Now she pitied herself and was ashamed. In addition she was ashamed of being ashamed.

Would you like to go shopping with me this afternoon? Beth said to Anna.

Anna did not answer.

We could go down to SoHo, said Beth.

Anna did not look up. She was wearing another of her father's shirts and a pair of old jeans and her sneakers.

I'm set, she said to her mother. I don't need anything.

Since when are clothes about need? said Beth.

Since now, said Anna.

If you stood on one side of the River Styx and looked across to the other you would see the shades milling about, going nowhere, sitting on rocks, standing under pale branches of emaciated trees. The shades were not so much ghosts of the living as imprints in space of bodies that had once pulsed with sinew and bone, fluids, waste, red blood, yellow urine, eyelashes, hair follicles, nails that grew and grew, teeth that sat in the gums until they didn't. Charon ferried the newly dead across the river to their eternal home. Fritz looked at Anna and saw that she was in her own boat, stranded in between the shores, floating in the river's current, but moving no closer to one shore or the other. She was a small figure far out in the waters. He had no boat. He waved, he signaled to her, row, row back toward me. She didn't hear him.

A new Woody Allen movie opened in the art theater on Broadway. Fritz asked Anna to go with him. No, she said. I don't like Woody Allen movies. How is that possible? said Fritz. On what planet are you living? he added. Not yours, she said and went into her room and closed the door.

3 a.m. It wasn't that Anna felt terrible. As she rinsed the towel she had used to blot the red blood that spurted from a particularly deep cut in her forearm, Anna noticed that she felt relief, peaceful, calm, ordinary, herself. It was as if she had vomited after a long nausea and now felt well again, her stomach settling back to its usual unannounced activities. It was odd, this peace that seemed to flow from her wounds, little wounds, almost pretend wounds, "just a game" wounds, but wounds.

Perhaps we should send her to one of those wilderness camps where they teach survival techniques if you're lost in the canyons or trapped in a landslide? he said to Beth. Fritz had looked them up online. He couldn't concentrate on his own research. He itched, he paced, he took quick naps, he worked out at the gym, he bought a new printer and then returned it. He reread T. S. Eliot. The poet was an anti-Semite and Fritz's anger rose, as new as the soft spot in a baby's head, as familiar as his own face in the mirror. And then he wrote an essay about the causes of anti-Semitism. He tore up his essay. He had nothing to say that hadn't been said a thousand times before. In the privacy of his office he considered that all the words he had written were washing away faster than he could write them. From dust to dust was not meant to refer to books, but how apt, how perfect a phrase, even if everything was digitized and the capacity of the machines was as large as the distance between earth and the sun or longer and wider, it wouldn't matter because the infinite collection of words, observations, pithy thoughts would soon become electronic waste, jumbled together, in long lines of zeros and ones, ignored by the living who would have other distractions, their own ones and zeros.

It was 11:15. The bell rang. Dr. Berman opened the door. The girl standing there looked familiar. She walked into the office and sat down in the patient's chair. She must be a patient, but who? The appointment book was across the room on her desk. Dr. Berman took her own chair and looked expectantly at the girl, waiting for her to begin. Her name would come to her. Everything would return. It usually did. She would not panic. She could manage this session. The name began with an A, Aster, Abigail, Alice. No, she thought, not that. B, Betsy, Barbara, Brenda?

Anna said, I had a dream last night that Meyer was waiting outside my door with a steak knife and he wanted to stab me in the heart.

Meyer was who?

Dr. Berman said, You must hate someone. Who is it you hate?

Anna smiled, a small smile. She took the word *hate* as a gift, as a treasure passed from mother to daughter, as a kindness on the part of her therapist. Hate, she said. I do, I do hate someone.

Everyone hates, said Dr. Berman.

Anna smiled again. She said, I'm good at hating. I'm really good at hating.

three

There was a long list in Dr. Z.'s head of things he didn't believe. It was far longer than the list of things he did believe. It began with the resurrection of Jesus, the power of prayer, the good intentions of the state, the possibility of political salvation, the kindness of strangers, and went on to the pathos of Santa Claus and his reindeer and along the way it swept up all but the pursuit of happiness. Dr. Z. did believe in the pursuit if not in the possession of happiness.

On the other hand there were days, hours, long periods of time when he was happy. What that meant when he questioned himself was that he felt no need to be anywhere other than where he was. He had brought his desires for greater recognition, more public acclaim, more love, and more wealth to heel. His long face, his balding head seemed just the right one for his big body. He believed that the beast that was man would never change for the better but could always be worse than expected. This thought did not make him grieve. It was calming in its way. He expected no miracles and accepted the bloodlust of nature and the raw devouring needs of selves, his own included. However he suffered when his children were disappointed. He suffered *when his wife was threatened with mutating cells in her left breast. He suffered when his patients felt hopeless or alone. He would have said this suffering was a sign of life. Without it he would have been a walking corpse. He was not a walking corpse. This was proved when a beautiful young woman walked past him on her way to another table in a restaurant and his loins jumped up and a flush came to his face and he moved his napkin over the offending organ.*

She will have one, said Dr. H.

It's the third time, said Dr. Z.

Not unusual, said Dr. H.

She's afraid it will never happen, said Dr. Z.

I'm sorry, said Dr. H.

The loss of a baby is—, said Dr. Z.

Not a baby, said Dr. H.

Not yet, said Dr. Z.

I'm sorry, said Dr. H.

Ronit told me not to come over, said Dr. Z.

Just for now, said Dr. H.

She'll try again, said Dr. Z.

It will happen, said Dr. H.

Dr. H. was expecting a new patient. He was not nervous but he was alert as if the curtain in a theater was about to rise, the audience was settling down. The lights were slowly dimming. And he, ready, focused on the stage, hopeful. Left open on his computer screen on his desk, facing away from the patient's chair, was a recipe for Mediterranean lamb stew. Dr. H. cooked for his wife, for his friends, for the sheer pleasure of taste and smell and pride in his offerings. Dr. H. read recipes the way other men read the sports pages. Joy, it gave him joy. His children had learned to eat oysters and eel and turned up their small noses at things like pasta and cheese without a sprinkling of parsley or a portion of spicy sausage.

The patient was an older man, a widower, referred by his internist, who had, after many costly tests, found nothing to explain the man's stomach ailments, his headaches, and his lethargy.

In the first moments after he opened the door there would be an awkwardness, shyness on the part of physician and his patient, who was not yet his patient, was just a man in an office with a stranger who might become more than a stranger or might not. Dr. H. knew, because the internist had told him, that the man, Mike Wilson (Wilson changed from Winofsky), age seventy-two, had been a CBS journalist and then the producer of the nightly news on a cable channel and had also published four books for children. He had retired two years ago just after his wife had died.

As Dr. H. waited for the bell to ring he straightened his tie. A disheveled analyst might alarm an already disheveled patient.

And then he was there, in the soft chair, his umbrella in the basket outside the door, his white hair still thick and somewhat long. His face, his ruined face, bony and sad, marked by a bang on the chin from a fall from a tree in a distant Brooklyn boyhood. He looked at Dr. H. and swiveled his head. Like a camera scanning from left to right, he observed all the colors, all the objects, all the shelves of books, the rocking chair in the corner, the box of children's toys on a low chest.

I understand, said Dr. H., you haven't been feeling so well.

No, said his new patient. I haven't.

A woman, thought Dr. H., would now begin to speak. A man would wait to see if it was safe. A man would make sure the other man in the room would not be dangerous. A man would stay on his side of the wall until he could not any longer. Dr. H. said, I understand that you lost your wife.

Mike Wilson said, Her name was Lourdes. We were colleagues. We met in Buenos Aires.

Dr. H. saw that his patient's hands had lifted as if to hide his face and then lowered to his lap as the gesture was suppressed. Dr. H. asked if his patient was having trouble sleeping. He spoke in his softest voice. It had the quality of a dust-speckled moonbeam floating through the room. The voice said: safe, quiet, private, not like the park, not like a restaurant, not like your friend's living room, but something else, a hiding place, without noise, a place where thought was sacred and an attempt would be made, a valiant attempt (be brave, patient, or would-be patient, of mine) to speak the truth, to rush after the truth, to force it from its hiding places.

Mike Wilson said, I would be willing to die now. I've had a full life. I don't need more. This was a statement. It was not dramatic. It was said the way a person speaks of the rain and mentions that he has forgotten his umbrella.

Dr. H. nodded, Often, after a great loss people find it hard to continue.

Silence.

Dr. H. said into the silence, Tell me about your wife.

Mike Wilson's internist had referred him to both a male and a female doctor. He had chosen the male. Perhaps that was a mistake.

It had been a year, Mike Wilson explained that he was tired, tired by ten in the morning, but of course that was because he couldn't get to sleep until the sinking moon appeared outside his window and no sleeping aid seemed to work for more than a few days.

How did your wife die? asked Dr. H.

Mike Wilson answered swiftly, the way you respond to the

customs officer on your return to the United States, no plants, no foods, no purchases over a few hundred dollars.

She died of lung cancer at home. We had excellent hospice care.

Only the drumming of fingers on the arm of the chair indicated that there was more to say, much more to say, but Dr. H. knew that would come. Inside his own chest he felt a dull ache, a wish to spare himself, a desire to get out of his chair and pace the room. He said, Tell me how she died. Were you with her?

And Mike Wilson told him about his son and daughter-in-law and told him about his other son who had not been able to come to the funeral, reasons to be explained later. He told him about the bottles of oxygen and the last thing that Lourdes had said to him: something to do with a soccer goal she had scored in high school.

Melancholy, loss, mourning, pathological or not—was there really a "not"? Dr. H. knew more about the subject than he would tell his patient. He knew enough to say almost nothing. Mike Wilson fell into the silence and said, I've been in three war zones, I've seen people die before. You see it immediately, the skin turns pale, the body is empty of itself, you know it, no question.

That's true, said Dr. H., but there are still a lot of questions to ask.

I know all the answers, said Mike Wilson.

Dr. H. said, If you did you would be sleeping.

Mike Wilson said, I've lost my appetite: not just for food.

Dr. H., I think you might want something else before you die.

I'm seventy-two, said Mike Wilson. And I've had enough.

Are you a gambling man? Mike Wilson asked Dr. H.

Silence.

You want to make a bet I don't live to Thanksgiving?

What year? asked Dr. H.

This year, said Mike Wilson.

You know the odds? asked Dr. H.

Mike Wilson smiled. This was a good game.

I don't bet, said Dr. H., ending the game.

There are days and months and years ahead, not as many as there once were, but enough to appreciate. It could be good to be alive.

It won't, said Mike Wilson, but nevertheless he agreed to meet with Dr. H. and try. All he had to lose was time and money. He had nothing better to do with his time and the money he had in the bank. The trip he and Lourdes were planning to take to the Norwegian fjords, the trip they had postponed until it was too late, that trip would be transformed into visits with Dr. H. Also, there was that other money, the money he wouldn't touch, in the safety deposit box, not his exactly, deep in the steel vault, two stories down from the street, a secret he vowed to keep from Dr. H.

Mike Wilson wanted to die, but not quite yet.

Mike Wilson dreamt he was in the studio and they were on-air and suddenly the anchor, Rory Cane, a man with wide lips and weary black eyes, began to whisper, and his voice got lower and lower and no one could hear him and the technicians were rushing around and sparks were flying from the wires strung from klieg lights and then the anchor took off his jacket and there was blood on his shirt. Someone had shot him.

Who shot him? asked Dr. H.

I don't know, said Mike Wilson. He was a good guy. He hadn't said a word against Mohammad or expressed any opinion on any matter at all. He was known to cheat at poker and a few people held it against him but I doubt they would shoot him.

Yes, said Dr. H.

He did once put his arm around Lourdes when we were covering the convention in Anaheim.

And? said Dr. H.

I didn't mind, said Mike Wilson. I didn't own her.

Uh-huh, said Dr. H.

You want to prescribe something for me? asked Mike Wilson. I have no objection to mind-altering drugs.

How much are you drinking? asked Dr. H.

Not enough, said Mike Wilson, not as much as when I was in Kuwait.

I'll prescribe something, said Dr. H., but think of it as a thin blanket, hardly enough to keep out the frost, not enough to keep your heart pumping, just enough to let us talk.

All right, said Mike Wilson. But nothing was all right.

Lourdes wore her hair loose and long. It went down to the middle of her spine. It was dark brown and soft and her nose was too wide and too long but her eyesight was perfect and she missed nothing. She could get angry quickly and just as quickly her anger turned to lust or affection, or song. I could bring you a photograph, said Mike Wilson.

Just tell me, said Dr. H., I prefer your words.

Lourdes liked to frighten me by swimming too far out in the sea. She was a good swimmer but sometimes I could hardly see her and the waves were high and loud.

Lourdes ran every morning in the park. She often smelled of sweat and soap and her legs were strong enough to hold me down on the bed and no matter how I struggled she wouldn't let me up until I—. Mike Wilson stopped. This was not the sort of thing you talked about.

Dr. H. said, Tell me more about her.

Mike Wilson stopped talking. He felt a great pressure on his chest. Was he having a heart attack? He felt a hot flash on his face, a grief came over him and there were no words to describe it, no words that he could form in his throat, his non-cooperating tongue was still and he would have been weeping, if he was the sort of man who wept, instead he coughed, he shook his head from side to side, he seemed to have let out a sound, perhaps a sigh, but it was involuntary, and he rejected the sound he heard coming from his own body.

There was silence in the room. The analyst waited and the patient knew the analyst was waiting and he wished he could speak but he couldn't.

The analyst said, What would Lourdes have wanted for you after her death? Did you talk about it?

Mike Wilson said, She said she wanted me to be happy.

And did you believe her? asked Dr. H.

I don't know, said Mike Wilson.

It was six months later when Mike Wilson told Dr. H. that his second son, Ivan, had been out of touch with his parents for five years. He was out of the country, living under a different name, unable to call or write. He had done something ungodly, this son who went to a private school on the Upper West Side and had excellent grades, played tennis on the school team, went on to his second choice college which was fine enough in New England and was gifted, really gifted, Mike Wilson assured Dr.

H., in math, and then he got a job with a firm downtown, a very prominent firm.

Ivan had a slight tic in his left eye, he had a love of jazz and he played the drums in a band he had formed with some friends. He was an ordinary boy, said Mike Wilson. He never took drugs or at least only the usual ones at parties. He didn't have a drinking problem, at least as far as we knew. He had a girlfriend from a rich family. They had a penthouse apartment on Fifth Avenue and a house in Sag Harbor, maybe that was it, the boats in the bay, he loved her boats.

Dr. H. was beginning to be able to guess the end of this tale. He said nothing.

It was in the *New York Post*. It was in *The New York Times*, at first just in the business section but then it moved on to the first page. Ivan was the youngest of those indicted. In telling the story Mike Wilson stopped himself from making the excuses he used with close friends, with Lourdes. It was the culture of greed, it was the opportunity that couldn't be resisted. Everyone was doing it. The excuses did not seem convincing in Dr. H.'s office. Ivan disappeared before the trial. He forfeited the bail his girlfriend had posted. In the following year Mike and Lourdes read that she was married to a prominent novelist and had moved to Wyoming.

Wherever he was, Mike said, he had missed his mother's funeral. He probably didn't know she had died. He probably didn't know how much she had hoped he would appear in the last weeks by her bedside.

So, said Dr. H., you have had two losses, not just one.

Ivan is not dead, said Mike Wilson.

Dr. H. said nothing.

But he might as well be, said Mike Wilson into the room. His voice bitter, strong, not that of a grieving man but that of an aggrieved man, betrayed by his son and abandoned by his wife (through no fault of her own).

After the session, on his way home, he was not thinking of his own death. He was not the sort of man to kick a small animal but he considered it as a stray cat crossed in front of him and dashed under the wheels of a parked car. Filthy beast, he thought as he passed.

He thought he might write a memoir. He had been around a good many floods, some hurricanes and political campaigns, funerals of presidents, and there was the war in Lebanon and the Kuwait desert. He knew what it felt like to wake up every day smelling like mold and fungus, the aftertaste of spices and alcohol, headache, lice in the hair, excited, ready, as if he were in a movie and celluloid-immortal. There, over there, he was always close to someone, a fellow journalist, a subject giving an interview, a child sitting on the curbside, and the sound of tanks moving and something in the sky, always lurking, ready to kill. He liked it. And then there was the Austrian photographer, Hannah, who now possessed his sweatshirt, a very small chip of his heart, and continued to exist in his mind for erotic purposes, now especially when he had the entire bed to himself all night long. Now that he was guilt-free or as guilt-free as a civilized man can be.

Dr. H. had said, You don't cheat on the dead by living.

It was kind of him to say that, but of course it wasn't true.

Lourdes had complained, he hadn't wanted to come back, to take a promotion, to stay in the city and be safe. He had little interest in safety. He did it for her and for Jeff, his oldest son, and for Ivan, Ivan-the-lost and Ivan-the-guilty, the bond money gone, Ivan.

Dr. H. considered his patient, the father who had never had a conscious criminal thought in his head. He considered the mother who had once stood outside the school doors waiting for her child to run up the steps. From her office phone she arranged his membership in the West Side Soccer Club. She made his dentist appointments and arranged for the babysitter to take him and his older brother to a music class, or a baseball practice or a play date with another boy who would also wear a Spider-Man costume on Halloween. What was missing in this boy that he could not resist the lure of easy money? Or was it something dangerous in the world that had caused the shards of glitter to fall into his heart, causing him to do the illegal thing for the reward of a bauble, an apartment, a suit of armor made of champagne corks, a place in the sun in a gated community that his father or his older brother could never afford and had never wanted.

Mike Wilson took Lourdes' scarves out of her drawer. He had not touched them since her death. They were long and silk and some had flowers and some had geometric lines, black and white they appeared to be a mathematician's dream.

Lourdes, went back to work a year after Ivan was born. She had been in a consciousness-raising group and one after another the woman began to receive paychecks and she was not the first or the last. She had taught calculus in a girls' school until March before her death. Her colleagues had come to the funeral and kissed him on the cheek or squeezed his hand and said they would miss her. Yes, yes, he had said, and was relieved when he knew their names.

She wore the scarves in her hair, or she wore them with her black coat. She wore them the way a parrot wears its tail, they just came with her every day. He would give them all to his daughter-in-law. She wouldn't wear them but she would keep them, in honor of Lourdes. He wanted to honor Lourdes. He would give this daughter-in-law the wedding ring, the simple band with a single diamond chip set into the gold. She had her own wedding band but it was time, it was important now to get that wedding band out of his chest of drawers, to move it on to another place. It weighed on him in the drawer.

He would not look at the photograph albums (his married son did not have leather-bound albums, he had online photos on his desktop). He didn't want to see his boys at the beach the summer they rented a mosquito-filled house in Fire Island. He didn't want to see lost teeth and birthday cakes and team trophies. He didn't want to see time slipping away. He especially didn't want to see Ivan, his slightly bucktoothed smile waving to the camera at his brother's engagement party. He especially didn't want to see Ivan whom he would never see again. He didn't want to see Ivan who belonged in jail, had been sentenced in absentia to ten years, who had disappeared and forfeited the bail money that had been posted by his girlfriend. He didn't want to think about Ivan at all but a man can't choose his thoughts and Ivan unbidden came again and again.

I'm haunted, he told Dr. H.

Too bad I'm not an exorcist, said Dr. H.

You could try, said Mike Wilson.

And what demon was it exactly that had run away with the boy that Ivan had been, citing the stats of every New York Yankee since 1921, unable to eat if his beloved Giants lost a game?

Mike Wilson's great-grandfather had danced at the Yom Kippur ball as the nineteenth century was ending. That night he had kissed the seamstress who would become his wife. On a tenement rooftop, under a scratchy wool blanket, the September air still warm, he had sent his genes into a welcoming place and those genes would be American, free of accent, free of shame. His story from that point onward would be the story of Pilgrims and Indians and of flags on the ramparts still standing. American history was itself just a few hundred years old, not thousands of years, like his old history, which had grown wretched and patched and useless as his own father's tattered texts muttered into an indifferent sky over Vilna, Vilna, a stopover in the years of exile: a burden to carry in the age of reason. Mike Wilson's great-grandfather hoped that his grandchildren would live in a town where no one could recall Job's name or identify with his fate. Justice, equality, decent wages, indoor plumbing, it all seemed possible.

That was the cartoon version. The real story had something to do with brothers quarreling and tuberculosis and a failed hardware business and two children buried in the city of the dead in outer Queens and a wife who was the kind of mother who hit her children whenever the mood came on her. Mike Wilson only knew that his own mother had been kind and dreamy and loved crossword puzzles and mystery stories and his own father had wanted to be a pilot but had become a schoolteacher and no one in the family had been in court for more than a traffic ticket and Ivan's arrest had not simply been a matter of public shame, but of private despair.

Dr. H. considered the question of Ivan. There was an explanation for the crime, another side of the story. The young man possessed a soul that had its reasons. Dr. H. preferred to understand rather than judge. Nevertheless he did not admire the behavior of this young man. Was he a capitalist pig or a hungry child who stumbled and broke apart? Why did he fall? Was this the old question of Adam in the garden? Or was it a gene missing a twist, or burdened with an extra curl. Dr. H. knew enough to avoid the problem of good and evil especially when it came to his patients and their children.

In fact he was angry at Ivan, on behalf of his father and his dead mother and perhaps of all those who didn't cheat. Ivan came in multiples, Ivan was many Ivans and they all had big bank accounts. Everywhere in the city, money was flowing and falling and changing hands and there was a race going on, a race for the best, most expensive view of the park or the river, there was a pounding on the doors of the stores on Madison Avenue where a hairbrush cost as much as a bus driver's monthly salary. There were tuitions and clothes and china plates and labels that meant something to those who wore them and the city was rippling with anxiety over who had everything and who had nothing and who would gain more and how to show what one had and how to keep it safe and make it grow and how to be better, a better bigger house in the country, a better bigger home theater, a better bigger cash flow, in and in and in. This was a city in which little children compared the monetary value of their birthday presents. Dr. H. sighed. He himself sometimes regretted not becoming a heart surgeon. Sometimes he too wanted to be able to fly first class to China and satisfy all his wants, one after another. There was a particular range stove he would have liked that cost as much as a small airplane.

Accumulation, competition, this was the addiction that humbled the city, that caused it to tremble in the predawn hours, the stench of avarice came off both rivers and wore down the citizens of the city, who scrambled like ants building their mountain of grains, fearing always the foot that would smash, the hand that would hammer, the end of the game.

If one thought of it, money was not so much the root of all evil but the air one breathed, the source of life itself, the energy that turned the wheels that made the city run day after day. Cash was needed not for survival but for flash and bravado, for astonishment and amusement, for security, a goal that kept receding into the mists as you came closer. Security was not a Swiss bank account. It was a state of mind as illusive and fleeting as joy. Once upon a time it was enough if you could feed your family. Now you needed to have more than your neighbor, who must therefore have less.

In his office with his bookshelves spilling over with old copies of the journals and the periodicals and the volumes of biography and the collected papers and the dusty whisper they seemed to make if you listened carefully, Dr. H. felt like a garage mechanic, a psychoanalytic garage mechanic, outside his little cell, shoes with spike heels cost as much as a racehorse, and money, the flow of it, the feel of it, the terror of losing it, fueled the motors of the real world, a world in which bundling did not mean cuddling and deals were cut with very sharp scissors. In that world his office, the little office of Dr. H. was of no importance at all.

Far away from Mount Eden, the cemetery where Lourdes was buried, sat the golden statues in the Vatican storehouse as well as the Picassos, the Matisses, the Andy Warhols that were hung on the walls of the princes of Wall Street. Yes, dreams were the royal road to the unconscious, but the unconscious, even under the analyst's keen eye, was not an item you could buy or sell. Dr. H. regretted that he lived in relative poverty. He regretted that money and its rewards had passed him by. No, he didn't regret that. What he minded was that all he held dear was less valued than it had been. Insight, thought, nature itself, affection, all seemed like fourth prizes in a contest he had not chosen to enter, but was in nevertheless. The devil stole away Mike Wilson's child and stuck his finger in Dr. H.'s eye.

Dr. H. did not accept his own dark thoughts as the complete truth. Perhaps they were a product of some shame of his own. He believed in personal responsibility.

He believed in choice and he believed that Ivan might not be lost forever because you never know, not really, what might happen, unlikely as it seems, Ivan could return and redeem his days. Psychoanalysts are not seers or prophets, not judges, not makers or shakers. If all goes well they may be able to work like sheep dogs and round up a few strays and press them back into the herd.

There was a day when Mike Wilson thought while eating a stale croissant at Starbucks, I lost my wife and my son but I have Dr. H. As long as I can pay for him, I have Dr. H. And by now he knew that Dr. H. was also a stand-in for his own father, brother, son, wife, mother, and something of a shape-shifter inhabiting his imagination while still knowing exactly how long forty-five minutes lasted, while knowing exactly the many ways Mike Wilson had to deceive himself and knowing how much regret a man could bear without breaking into fragments that could never be put back together again.

At least Mike Wilson hoped that was so. Perhaps it wasn't.

Are you hoping that your son will contact you one day when he feels enough time has gone by? said Dr. H.

It has been six years, said Mike Wilson. I call his old friends from high school. I call his college roommate every six months. I call his old girlfriend who hangs up on me. If this were a movie, I'd find a clue. A phone call would come at three in the morning with a stranger whispering a country name, an address into the air. I would open an unmarked envelope and find a blank page and then notice the stamp, the country of origin. But I am not hoping.

Dr. H. said, Hope will not harm you.

Mike Wilson sat in the leather chair opposite Dr. H. and wanted to tell him, wanted to tell someone, about the volcano that sat in his breast sending fire and ash up into his brain. The lava that flowed down from that volcano, the lava that was the dark hot stuff of his love for his child, his child who had done a criminal thing, his child whom he would never see again.

You are angry at him, said Dr. H.

Yes, said Mike Wilson, who actually was exhausted, bone-achingly exhausted from loss. How angry can an exhausted man get?

I'm too old, said Mike Wilson, to have another child.

Not too old, said Dr. H., to have another wife.

I don't want another wife, said Mike Wilson. The idea of another woman made him want to smash his head into the wall, the one with Dr. H.'s poster of the Sistine Chapel that he had picked up at an international psychoanalytic meeting in Florence. Did Dr. H. identify with God and that outstretched arm?

Absolutely not.

On rare occasions only.

Dr. H. knew that his patient did not know his own mind, that is the way it was with patients.

Lourdes had sat through every day of the trial. She stared at the jury, memorizing all their faces. She did not insist as the lawyer did that her son was innocent, but she hugged him in front of the reporters so they would know that this man was not an outlaw but someone's beloved child. Of course he was also an outlaw, an anti-Robin Hood, who had robbed the poor to serve the rich.

Do you ever think, asked Dr. H., that Ivan and his troubles gave Lourdes lung cancer?

No, said Mike Wilson, of course not. But then he said into the waiting silence, It may have made her vulnerable, broken some resistance, made her not want to breathe.

And one day he said to Dr. H., Maybe it was Lourdes' fault. Maybe she loved him too much and spoiled him, so he thought he could get away with anything. She thought he was perfect. He probably believed her. There was a hint of a whine in Mike Wilson's voice.

Did you say that to her? asked Dr. H.

No, said Mike Wilson.

But there it was in the room, the son and the father, and the eternal Oedipus that must be endured for all to survive with 20/20 vision. Dr. H. heard it as if a gong had struck on a mountaintop and the echo slowly drifted down into the valley below. The father, a mere mortal, had sometimes been jealous of his son, in the way that fathers and sons have wrestled from the beginning of time. There was in Ivan's flight some fragment of victory for the journalist who was himself away from his hearth for many months, leaving the mother and the son to themselves. It would take a long time and multiple gentle hints before Mike Wilson might see this himself, but Dr. H. would try in time, because he believed it was true and truth was the antibiotic of the mind.

We were in Memorial Sloan Kettering hospital waiting for her name to be called. We were in a beautiful room with a view of the river outside. I went to get a Coke from the machine in the hall and when I came back Lourdes said, I'm done and I said all right. Maybe I shouldn't have said that. Mike Wilson looked at Dr. H. He was ready to catch any expression on his face that might tell him if he had been negligent, ignorant, selfish. He had of course been all those things. Did Dr. H. think he was a dishonorable man?

If he did it didn't show on his face.

Why should he care what Dr. H. thought of him? He shouldn't. But he did. He was tied to Dr. H. who was insisting he live, who wanted him to live, and so he would live for a while, because Dr. H. was trying so hard to keep him above ground, where Mike Wilson had to admit the possibilities were not all bad, at least not yet.

And then Dr. H. announced that he was taking a vacation in early April. There would be missed appointments. Money saved, thought Mike Wilson, although he would have preferred it if Dr. H. had remained in his office. Of course he knew that Dr. H. had a life of his own, maybe a family with children, but it still seemed wrong of him, to so easily take a vacation. He himself did not want to go anywhere. Where would he go, a man alone.

The air became warmer, there were some buds on the trees in the park, there were lilacs in the buckets at the markets on Broadway. There were more skateboards on the streets. The restaurants were putting tables and chairs on the sidewalks.

Dr. H., his wife and son and daughter went to Belize. The palm trees were everywhere. The houses were pink and blue and along the road from the airport to their hotel on the shore, noses pressed against flimsy fences, donkeys watched the cars go by.

In the hotel lobby as they were checking in, Dr. H. saw the sign for a flat-bottom fishing trip, a photo of a huge tarpon decorated the poster, a four-hour trip, leaving at 6 a.m. His heart jumped. Yes, he wanted to do that. Yes, he loved fishing which his wife thought revolting and cruel. His son would come and he would, he would do it. His daughter refused. She was not yet eight. She felt sorry for the fish. Was it cruel? He preferred to eat what he caught. But the truth was that he liked the long wait for the hit on the end of the line. He liked the joy that jumped in his chest as he reeled in the shinning creature, scales, blank eyes, thrashing and struggling for its life. He liked the victory. He liked the murder. He liked the taste, he liked the sight of the fish in the bottom of the boat, his fish, his catch. I'm not a saint, he said to himself, and that was that.

His wife worked for a nonprofit, raising funds for tutoring programs in the inner city. She volunteered at an organization that arranged for the children of incarcerated drug dealers to go to the circus or spend a few weeks at a summer camp. On the beach in Belize she forgot the forlorn and the downtrodden and danced at night in her husband's arms, and helped her children collect shells and allowed her daughter to place a live crab on her thigh, and wore a bikini that made her husband grab her from behind and hold on so long that his son complained, Let go Dad, which made his wife laugh, which made him happy.

In bed at night she said to him, Maybe we should move here.

Maybe we shouldn't, he said.

There must be a great need on this island for psychoanalysts, she said.

Sure, he said.

I'm thinking, she said, you could go back to real medicine, you could be a GP and take care of the natives and the tourists: stomachaches and sunburn.

Tempting, he said.

I'm sure they could use you, she said. She wasn't serious.

I wish, he said, I could have been Dr. Salk. I wish I had been the one to discover the polio vaccine but since I was born too late I think I'll just continue to see my patients.

Are you bored? she asked. Are you ever bored?

No, he said, and then the Tequila Sunrise hit him and he closed his eyes and fell instantly asleep.

At breakfast she said to him, You're my hero.

Sure, he said.

You don't have doubts? She pinched his arm.

About what? he asked.

Oh you know, she said.

His youngest child took a running leap into the pool. Look at me, said the child.

I'm looking, he said, turning back to his wife. If a small splash of human happiness is added to the atmosphere, then I have been of use. If I remove a pain, an unnecessary fear, unblock the repression, undo the guilt, pull someone out of the cave they are hiding in, then I am doing as well as can be expected.

All right, she said, and put her third croissant with strawberry jam into her mouth.

Maybe we should invite my mother for dinner when we get back, she said.

Do you want to go water-skiing this afternoon? he said.

And two days later, his face somewhat pink despite the sunblock his wife had smoothed across his nose again and again, his arms beginning to tan, his tenth attempt to read *Remembrance of Things Past* not yet abandoned, he was on the dock where the boat waited as the sky blushed with morning sun and the white sliver of a dying moon was about to fall into the distant turquoise sea. The captain of their fishing boat shook his hand, patted the boy on his shoulder, and asked them to sit down as they motored out to the flats. On the shore the palm trees bent and cast their shadows on the sand and his wife opened her eyes, happy not to be fishing, happy he was fishing, happy to feel the warm air on her arms, and wondered if she was too old to have another child. Maybe not.

The captain had an assistant, a native boy who put bait on the hooks, who showed them how to cast far out into the waters, who took the bonefish that the boy caught and placed it on a bench and banged its head in with a hammer and tossed it into a bucket. The captain said his name was Harry and he was an American who had come to Belize because he wanted to live on the water, and he owned this boat and two others. The sky was cloudless. The morning was perfect.

Dr. H. had a tarpon on his line. It circled the boat again and again in an attempt to break the line. Clever tarpon, its desire to live churning up the aqua sea, fierce and unyielding, until one hour and twelve minutes later, exhausted, it rose against the boat's side. Good work, said Captain Harry, who had given instructions the entire time and probably deserved the credit for the capture. The tarpon was released back into the water. You don't have to eat or kill everything in the sea, said Captain Harry, and there was something in the way he spoke, the rhythm of the words, that caught Dr. H.'s attention. And then he looked carefully at the fisherman and he saw that his face was familiar, not exactly like the one he knew, but similar. Was it the curve of the mouth? Was it the nose which was longer than many but not unusual? Was it something in the smile? Had his patient mentioned overlapping front teeth? Captain Harry's eyes were hidden behind dark sunglasses. Were those glasses hiding a tic? Of course that was ridiculous, the odds of such a thing were impossible.

Where did you grow up? Dr. H. asked as the boat seemed to glide across the shallow waters. Not here, said Captain Harry. Where? said Dr. H. North, said Captain Harry, where it snowed.

I hated the snow. Captain Harry turned to his ropes and his reels that rested in holders clipped to the gunnels of the boat. Of course it was ridiculous. He was imagining, he was losing distance between himself and his patient. He would have to examine his overidentification with his patient. It was absurd but he couldn't get it out of his mind.

The boat moved close to the shore of an island, covered in thick green ferns, palms, birdsong overhead, birds fighting, a spitting sound above. There were rocks beneath, and schools of small colored fish darted behind waving underwater plants. In the branches of a palm tree on the nearby shore his son saw a red and golden parrot. Hey look at that, Dad, he said, and pointed.

And Dr. H., without thinking, without calculation, said loudly to the captain who had his back turned, Ivan, what kind of parrot is that? And the captain turned around, frightened, amazed, a tension in his shoulders. Harry, he said, my name is Harry.

Six days later, early on the morning that they were scheduled to leave for the airport and the return trip to New York, Dr. H., having carefully weighed the pros and the cons of what he was about to do, walked to the dock and saw the boat waiting at the end and Captain Harry drinking coffee from his thermos and his assistant piling soft drinks into the cooler for the customers who would soon arrive, a lawyer and his girlfriend who was somebody else's wife, but who cared in the forgiving warmth of the new daylight.

Dr. H. walked down to the edge of the dock. He took a bulky letter he had written on hotel stationery out of his pocket and handed it to the captain who had turned his back when he saw him approaching but his way was blocked. Captain Harry took the letter and later, after he had brought the lawyer and his girlfriend back to the dock, after he had washed the smell of terrified tarpon off his calloused hands, he opened the envelope.

Ivan, it said, call your father. He needs you. And inside the letter was a cell phone, which if anyone traced would come back to Dr. H. sitting in his office in New York City, who would claim he had lost his cell phone on a vacation in Belize. Inside the small perfect phone was a listing of only one patient, all the other numbers had been erased. Mr. Mike Wilson's address and number were there for Ivan.

Of course he shouldn't have done that, Dr. H. scolded himself as soon as he had fastened his seat belt and pulled *Remembrance of Things Past* out of his carry-on bag. Analysts do not interfere in their patients' real lives. It spoils the work. It changes everything. It isn't professional. And perhaps he was wrong, in which case the countertransference, the over-involvement, would not matter very much and be washed out to sea like a leftover plastic glass holding the remains of a Tequila Sunrise with its little paper parasol covered in wet sand.

How was your vacation? asked Dr. Z.

And Dr. H. told him, No real names used.

Wishful thinking, said Dr. Z.

No, said Dr. H.

Magical thinking, said Dr. Z.

No, said Dr. H.

four

It wouldn't be polite to ask Dr. Berman if she was listening. He was sitting opposite her in the patient's chair but he was not a patient. He was a young analyst and he had his own analyst, the newly appointed head of the education committee at his institute, Dr. H., whom he had just seen several hours before. Dr. Berman was the young analyst's supervisor. She was supposed to listen to his reports of an analytic patient he was working with and to offer advice and comment on his technique, to deepen his thoughts, to help him, help the patient. It was a good system. The older analyst could see around the corners that the younger analyst could not. Also the older analyst could provide protection and support for the younger in the institute and so create opportunities for him to become a training analyst himself, the head of various faculty committees, to join the international organization, to hold prominent positions in the American Psychoanalytic Association. Ultimately, if he did creative work he himself could be the one who gave opening speeches at meetings, who was respected or feared by his colleagues. Dr. Berman could be, if all went well, his psychoanalytic mother. Or she could not. He knew he had a few long years of work ahead of him before he would be certified to work on his own.

Analysis is not a romance novel. *She lived happily ever after with the love of her life in his castle by the sea and developed a vaccine that prevented river blindness* was a result to be devoutly pursued but most improbable. The end was more modest, more attainable than that. The end of the analysis would approach when the patient could manage to travel through the debris of his or her past and nod in its direction as it attempted to interrupt the pursuit, the daily boring pursuit of happiness that is all of our right to seek. The young analyst knew that but like a person learning a new language he had to repeat it to himself several times a day.

The young analyst understood that the rest of the world did not think so well of analysts. His own brother who was a physics professor at a university in Minnesota was convinced, and repeated his conviction at every family occasion, that the entire Freudian idea and all its offshoots and its incessant babble was without scientific basis and as dated as their grandfather's pocket watch. The young analyst was not swayed. This is what he wanted to do. This is what interested him. It might be alchemy. The gold it produced might be mere copper, but it had caught him and held him tight. His brother teased him. You could have gone to India and walked about bald, barefoot in an orange robe with a begging cup. At least you would have been earning an honest living. The young analyst went right on. If he was in a cult, so be it. If his work became totally irrelevant because pharmacology replaced him with a cheap cure that came in a bottle, it would have been worth it, worth it for him and he believed, despite his brother, for his patients.

But today, Dr. Berman had a gray pallor and her lipstick did not appear to be applied carefully. She had turned her head to look out at the park. Had he been boring? Had he said something so wrong that she had simply blocked out the rest of his words? He waited for her to turn toward him. She did not. Dr. Berman, he finally said, shall I go on? There was no answer. He leaned forward in his seat. Are you all right, Dr. Berman? he said loudly.

She startled. She turned toward him. Whatever you just said, say it again, she snapped. She was back with him, he hoped.

She talks about her ex-husband's love of Renaissance painting. She talks about his hands, how they make shapes in the air when he speaks. She does not talk about his wanderings at night, although she told me he often left the bed after midnight and didn't return until dawn. I asked her what she thought he was doing. She said she had no idea. She talks about her more beautiful sister, who remains more beautiful, but when I ask her about her dreams she says she has none. When I ask her to tell me about her childhood, she tells me how good she was at archery, and that she had the lead in her high school production of *The Sound of Music*. I ask if she thinks about me between sessions. She says not at all.

And then I ask her why her husband left. And she weeps and she weeps and she says she has no idea. None? I ask. She weeps. He is living, she tells me, with a roommate in Boston. I ask her what attracted her to him when they first met. Did you desire him? I asked. She wept. I don't know if that was a yes weeping or a no weeping.

Dr. Berman says, Don't use words like *desire*. Say what you mean. Did she want to have sex with him when they met? You use language that makes it possible for the patient to speak without the cover of social pretensions. Oh, said the young analyst. He sighed.

Dr. Berman responded to his sigh. Don't worry. You weren't born an analyst.

It often starts this way. She will tell you what you need to know in time. Just keep listening.

It's like listening to white noise, says the young analyst.

No, says Dr. Berman, it's like listening to the tide come in. Be patient, said Dr. Berman, something will wash up on the shore.

Go back to sex, says Dr. Berman. Perhaps she will tell you some moment, a boy's hand on hers, a sight of a couple kissing, something that began in the outside world and moved into her body, and she knew, at least for a moment, that sex was more than a word in a manual.

I think, said the young analyst, her longing is for a better wardrobe.

Dr. Berman did not smile. She said, Every woman wants a better wardrobe.

The young analyst was suddenly shy. What was he supposed to say?

You don't like this patient? Dr. Berman said to him.

I don't know her very well, he said.

You will, said Dr. Berman.

And what if then I don't like her? said the young analyst.

Then we will talk about you. If that happens the problem is yours to understand. We will look at your countertransference. It sounded to the young analyst like a threat but of course he knew countertransference was normal, a flow of his own emotional responses back into his consulting room, hanging over his patient, seeping into his every comment.

Dr. Berman put on her glasses and glanced at the clock on her desk and the young analyst gathered himself together and left.

Dr. Berman liked the young man. She wondered about his

own sexual history. Where was the crucible that drew him to his chosen profession? What had seared his brain? It would be good to know that, she thought.

As he walked down Central Park West back to his own office, the young analyst considered his patient. She had come to him because she couldn't sleep, because she was afraid of the dark and had kept all the lights on in her apartment since her husband had left. She had been an art history graduate student but had dropped out of the program after her marriage ended. Her parents were supporting her and wanted her to move to the Napa Valley where they had retired. She loved her parents, she said. She had a good childhood, she said. She seemed stunned, like a cartoon person hit on the head with a frying pan. He thought of her like Sleeping Beauty, a kiss would revive her. He was the prince, she was the comatose princess. This was one of those thoughts he would not tell his wife. He would tell Dr. H., but he wished that image had not drifted up into his consciousness. It should have stayed in the deep mud of his unconscious where it belonged.

The patient had a name, Lyla Shulman. She had a social security number and a driver's license: which should have been sufficient proof that she was not a character in someone else's story. One moment she had been an ordinary person. She picked out her wedding gifts at Bloomingdale's. Her mother had tears in her eyes when she tried on her bridal dress in the store. One moment she had been considering a thesis on Otto Dix and his use of bold dark, thick strokes, carrying, as her professor had pointed out, the hints of the Weimar Republic's infernal destination. The moment before that she had been fighting off Bobby Schwartz in the back of a taxicab on their way to a party in SoHo.

Her analyst seemed to be listening. She could almost feel him leaning forward in his chair, concentrating on her words. Of course that might not be true. He might be thinking of his own wife or their vacation plans or his child's crossed eyes. He might not have children. He wore a ring. She had noticed that when she came to consult him, recommended by the clinic at the institute that had itself been suggested to her by her cousin in New Rochelle who had promised her good results at less than the full rate. Her mother appreciated the discount.

When she walked through the park to his office she thought of herself as a figure in a Seurat painting. A shape formed by tiny specks of color that might separate off and go their own ways if the wind blew strongly or the painter decided she didn't belong on the canvas and preferred to put a tree in her place.

Now that her husband had left, at night she sometimes fixed herself a frozen dinner and then went out for a walk. She would look up at the sky, or what she could see of it between the buildings on Lexington Avenue, and consider the billions of people on the planet and the miles to the moon and beyond and she would feel soothed by the very immensity of the universe. If she walked in front of a car, if she fell off a cliff in Montauk where they had been on their honeymoon, if she took all the pills in her medicine cabinet, no matter what, it would not matter. She was replaceable.

Sometimes this thought calmed her. Other times it made her tremble and go home and call her mother who would repeat her hope that her daughter would come to California. There was a room waiting for her. Her mother knew from experience that this invitation would be rejected and often rudely. Her mother suggested she adopt a cat or a dog from the rescue program. Lyla thought people who lavished love on dumb beasts were pathetic. Anyone can win an animal's affection by serving up kibble day after day. Lyla wanted more. Lyla wanted her analyst to love her even though she knew that was out of the question, outside the rules, the worst possible outcome of a therapy. On the other hand it might be the best possible outcome.

The young analyst wanted to help Lyla Shulman rejoin her life and grow into a vibrant woman. The young analyst did believe that loving someone was essential to mental health. Or at least holding on to the hope that one might love and be loved was essential. In addition he wanted to impress Dr. Berman with his skill. He also wanted his own analyst, the often inscrutable Dr. H., to be pleased, pleased and admiring.

But what was love? He knew it began in infancy. He knew it was mixed with fear of loss, terror of separation, and he believed that there could be no love without anger at the loved one, who must disappoint, who is never good enough, not all the time. He knew that love had nothing to do with valentines and cupid and everything to do with sharp-tipped arrows often dipped in poison, the poison of memory, and the poison of helplessness.

No patient is boring, he had learned in one of his classes at the institute. It is you, the analyst, who is boring. Was this really true? Was he boring Lyla Shulman?

Some days lying on his couch holding on to her tissues as if they were small lifeboats bobbing in her sea of tears, Lyla would feel as if she were drowning in her own grief, as if there was no sandy bottom in this immense lake, as if she were Alice shrunken and paddling frantically in a sea of her own grief. Would her analyst say something before she went under for the third time or would he just sit there, a sunbather, on a shore she had no hope of reaching?

Sexual arousal, she heard the expression, before she made sense of it. Her analyst wanted to know if she had wanted her husband to enter her and what it had felt like and how was it when she first felt it. The tears stopped. She wanted to answer him, but what was the answer. I'm not sure, she said. The young analyst waited. He almost held his breath. He did not shift in his chair. Lyla said, I had to have a boyfriend.

Because? said the young analyst, not at all bored. And she told him and she told him and when the session ended he thought it had gone by too quickly. And one fact had come clear. Lyla Shulman had not desired her husband in the usual sense. Her desire more closely resembled something a woman must have like good teeth and clean hair. She had desired her husband to please her mother.

Sexual pleasure, thought the young analyst, how sad to live without it, without it rising in the nighttime, rising when watching the lovers in a movie kiss, when walking behind a woman with long legs and thin heels clicking on the sidewalk. How could it be someone like Lyla was not clear what he meant by sexual feelings? She knew the words but had not felt their consuming force. But the young analyst was not ashamed of his day's work and on his way home that evening he stopped and bought his wife a bottle of not too expensive Pinot Grigio. They would share it after the children were in bed and sexual lust, his awakened senses, would fill his mouth, his ears, would shine out from on the top of his head where his hair was already thinning, would come through his fingers onto her breasts and instinct, animal instinct, would carry him forward.

Later when he slept he had a nightmare. One that left him sweaty and kept him awake until morning. It is not easy to be happy, to be guilt-free, to keep anger caged in its zoo, and at night in one's sleep, the cages open, the rotten residue of memory rises and frolics, its malicious frolic, till dawn. This did not surprise the young analyst. He would tell Dr. H. about his dream.

What was sexual lust? It was the precursor of pornography, exploitation, whips and chains, screams and blood and at the same time it was the fuel of connection, affection, passion. A man with the best intentions could sometimes lose his way. A young woman like Lyla Shulman could learn to dance and dress in tight skirts and high heels and still miss the point. He wasn't allowed to just tell her that. He would have to wait until she told him.

The young analyst cut himself above his lip while he was shaving. Everyone needs a little punishment from time to time.

And so he considered Lyla Shulman. She was not hallucinating. She did not hear voices telling her that she was worthless, lazy, or criminal, like his first hospitalized patient whose eyes fixed on his face with a look of wild hope he couldn't bear, couldn't bear because he couldn't cure, couldn't change, couldn't write a different end to her story. He had made soothing noises—adjusted medications—felt broken himself, as if she had a contagious disease. Lyla was not like that. But all the same she might have needed a more experienced analyst. He knew that the more experienced analysts once were inexperienced.

Lyla was stalled. Lyla was dull. She had left the subject of sex behind but she would come back to it. Dr. Berman did not doubt that. Lyla was depressed but not in the way that called for an ambulance. He thought of his family cat Mookie stalking a bird in the garden, silently, slowly, one paw raised, stillness in all the muscles. He would be Mookie in the garden of his office.

He thought of a firecracker he and his brother had set off one July 4th on the Jersey Shore. It had made a whooshing sound, it had soared upwards, it had set off a few glowing lights in a pinwheel shape and then suddenly it had faded in the darkness a few feet above the dunes. His brother had said it was his fault but it wasn't his fault. Every firecracker does not succeed in lighting up the sky.

Words, words, if only his patient would use words and dry her tears and give him some material to work with. When he said that to Dr. Berman the following week, she said, Let her be sad, let her feel what she needs to feel. Dr. Berman spoke in a low, tired voice. She was disappointed in him, or she was tired. He wasn't sure.

Lyla considered Bruegel. She considered the painting of Icarus falling from the sky, his wax wings melted by the sun, while the peasants continued undisturbed to cut the hay, feed their horses, carry their vegetables in baskets to the market. Flowers bent their heads in the breeze while Icarus, unnoticed, fell and fell and died in the waters off the shore and if not for the artist, not for the poet, would have been forgotten, wiped away. She felt she was falling. She felt her wings had melted. She felt the water below, deep and lethal. She did decide to tell her analyst and see what he thought about Bruegel, about falling, about the great inattention of the world to the screaming boy headed downwards.

The young analyst had not seen the painting. He was pre-med after all. She described it well enough. He got the point. Do you think I don't see you? he asked.

Do you? she asked him. He waited.

Nothing.

Everyone is dying, she said.

But while they are dying they are living, he said. Was that a pompous thing to say? Maybe? The red button on his answering machine was flickering.

One afternoon as the light was fading in his office and the shadows were spreading across his oriental rug, the one he and his wife had bought on sale at a rug warehouse in New Jersey, Lyla said, My ex-husband likes men.

The young analyst considered asking her if she had hints of this before they got married. Instead he was silent, but sitting up very straight in his chair, leaning forward, willing her to speak.

Everyone is bisexual, Lyla said. I read that in *New York Magazine*.

Are you bisexual? the young analyst asked.

I told you already, she said. I am normal. Aren't you listening to me? she added in a tone that would have hurt his feelings if he didn't know that his feelings were part of the tool kit he would use to help his patient and were therefore welcome even when they were not welcome. Lyla Shulman told him her husband had always closed his eyes when she appeared nude before him. He told her, in the last days they had been living together, that he had discovered his true self, a self that could not be attracted to her. It wasn't personal. It was her gender. It's not my fault, she said. It is nobody's fault, said her analyst.

The young analyst heard his own heartbeat. The session was over at last. Her big secret, at least one of them, was his at last.

Lyla left his office spilling no tears. She left his office with a new thought. Maybe, she thought, I can, I will.

Dr. Berman was not pleased with his report. Sex, she said, you think that is all that this about.

No, he said, not at all. She interrupted him.

This young woman has locked herself up. Find her, release her, sex is just part of the story. For God's sake, she said, stop thinking about sex all the time. The young analyst blushed.

But sex was the subject of his next session with Lyla and the one after that and after that.

It had begun at a party at her best friend's house at a brownstone uptown. There was a small garden terrace with candle lights on little tables and chairs and she had gone outside to get away from the air conditioning which was too cold and there at one table her future husband was leaning back in his chair and his face seemed so perfect, like a Greek marble statue. It turned out that ancient Athens was just the right town for him. She should have paid more attention to the clue. Her analyst said that she did just that: pay attention.

One afternoon before her session, Lyla Shulman went to the museum. Perhaps she might pick up a man in the museum. She saw one just ahead of her in line to purchase a ticket. He was talking about something intently to someone just ahead of him. Lyla saw his face when he briefly turned around to glance at the revolving door. He was tall and his hair almost reached his shirt collar. Maybe he was a painter? Lyla thought about what she might say to him, to start the conversation. She considered tripping in front of him and apologizing. Then as he was leaving the counter he put his arm around the man he had spoken to, who was now waiting for him, and she saw that they were together. Had she known all along that her husband was just pretending an interest in her? Was this her choice? When her mother asked her, How is it going with the doctor? she answered, Fine thank you. When I next come to town, her mother said, I would like to meet with your doctor. Never, thought Lyla. Maybe, she said.

Good work, said Dr. Berman to the young analyst. But then she dismissed him twenty minutes early. He thought it would be rude to mention the time. He thought she might think he was greedy. He felt cheated. He was going to tell Dr. H. but he forgot about the twenty minutes she stole from him before his next appointment.

Dr. Berman left the hair salon with a red flush at the nape of her neck where the back of the sink had pressured her and the hair blower had been too hot. She stood on the street, the familiar street. She turned left toward Central Park. She stopped. Should she have turned right? She looked at the street signs but found no clue. She continued up the side street. It was a long block. It was a familiar block but should she have gone the other way? A fear came on her. It was the wrong way. She turned and retraced her steps. But when she got back to the corner she still wasn't sure. How was this possible? It was a passing confusion. Anyone could get turned around in a city where sirens wailed and buses wheezed and crowds pushed into markets and stores, and strollers, everywhere strollers crossing and recrossing streets. Dr. Berman stepped into the curb and hailed a taxi and gave the driver her address. It was only a ride of a few blocks but she was safe and as she stepped out of the cab and saw her own doorman on the steps of the building, she gave him a warm smile. He deserved the large gift she had placed in his envelope at Christmas time.

Lyla sat beside the window looking out at the building across the street. She saw a child running with something in his hand. In the next window she could see a woman who now bent down to the child. She could see neither of them anymore. She turned away from the window. She called a friend from school, now living in Boston, expecting her first child in a few months.

They spoke of another friend who had gone to Egypt with her boyfriend. No one had heard anything for months. People just disappear, said Lyla. Come and visit me, said her friend. I can't, said Lyla, I'm too busy just now. Masterpiece Theatre began, a rerun of Inspector Lewis, who never failed to find the murderer despite his lack of a university education. Lyla called her mother.

Through the cloud, into the atmosphere, riddled with electronic fragments, invisible to the naked eye, one coast to another, speech was carried, instantly. Or was that not right? Perhaps the spoken words were transported without bodies, or form, but like people in *Star Trek*, beamed across the mountains, re-formed in the ears of the people they were meant for, as words, or in her case as a call for a bedtime story, another glass of water, a holding on to the daylight as long as possible.

Nothing is happening, said the young analyst to Dr. Berman.
  Nothing you know about is happening, said Dr. Berman.
  What should I say? asked the young analyst.
  About what? asked Dr. Berman.

And then one morning Lyla Shulman said to her analyst, My mother thinks my sister is smarter than I am. And Lyla didn't weep. She said, She isn't. And then she said, She's nothing, nothing at all. The voice she used for this sentence startled her analyst. It was like an ice pick, sharp, made of unbreakable steel, a weapon to pierce and draw blood. Lyla had not mentioned her sister since their first meeting. Was she older or younger? He had forgotten. He could look at his original notes later or he could ask her right now. He made a decision. Tell me more about your sister, he said. And Lyla told him. She was older. She once pushed her in a closet and wouldn't open the door. That closet was a metaphor, the analyst knew. Soon enough he could say that to Lyla, but not yet. First he had to listen, as still as a small toad under a fern leaf, as the storm from the sea approached and the sky above the pines darkened and the cracks of lightning came closer.

And this worthless sister was a lawyer, a graduate of a top-ranked law school, who worked for a public interest firm that protected the interests of the homeless, the unfairly fired, those denied medical care, the illegals awaiting deportation. She had a husband who was a professor of archaeology and the author of a book whose title Lyla didn't remember. This professor had said to his mother-in-law that Lyla needed to grow up. That Lyla did remember. This sister, who had prevented Lyla from sitting on her mother's lap, from combing her mother's hair, from singing songs into her mother's ear, also had two little girls, one named Lyla. This sister, Lyla told her analyst, had very small breasts, the left smaller than the right.

This remark made the young analyst think about Lyla's breasts, which did not seem uneven or small.

And there it was, a thread to Lyla's soul. This thread would lead through the most ordinary of matters, tennis lessons, a school play, a fight with a girlfriend who had a crush on their teacher, and it would come to a hard hating place where jealousy and rage and the other demons of the soul would stamp and roar, not harmlessly, but with real fangs and claws that could cripple and destroy. And the young analyst wanted, wanted now with a ferocity he didn't know belonged to him, to bring Lyla to life, real life, with a life-sized sister and a way forward. This was everything; this was it, what his training was for, to add just one finite amount of good life to a person who might otherwise have missed their moment. It wasn't much, he knew. It wouldn't stop starvation or disease on the African continent. It wouldn't lift up the poor or save a single river from drying to dust, but it was his work, this little moment of freedom from the past, that he might be able to bring to Lyla Shulman, if he didn't make some clumsy mistake and she had the courage and the persistence to go on, and her mother kept paying for the treatment.

Lyla Shulman's mother was worried about Lyla. She had a whine in her voice. Lyla Shulman's mother recognized that whine. She thought her daughter had left it behind but there it was again, an aggrieved nostril wheeze. After the light was turned out and the dog had settled at the edge of the bed where he wasn't supposed to sleep but always did, Lyla Shulman's mother felt as if she were vanishing, despite being a size fourteen, and struggling not to go to sixteen. She thought of Lyla's birth, the pain she did not remember, although she had done it the Lamaze way, no medicine, no spinal tap, just nature moving her second and last baby down a canal, with some difficulty. The exhilaration, the pure unequaled exhilaration of the life created, the newness, the softness, the tiny hands, the red chapped lips, the sucking noises, and she was glad it was another girl. And now she felt defeated, defeated by enemies she could not see or hear. She did not know what to do about Lyla. There was in fact nothing to do about Lyla. And if Lyla was not content, then her mother—together with the billion small choices she had made over the years—was implicated in the fact of Lyla, less than happy, Lyla alone, Lyla divorced, Lyla adrift. Had she preferred Lyla's sister? Of course not. She sat up in bed and reached for the heavy novel on the night table. Her book club was reading *War and Peace*. Her husband was sound asleep.

Lyla would have to do it, whatever it was, herself: with the help of her young and very eager, maybe too eager, analyst.

Lyla Shulman told her analyst something very private. Something she would not say to a friend or a date or even her mother. She wanted to be famous. She didn't know for what or how to start. How jealous that would make her sister. There is nothing special in me, she said. It's safer to think that, said her analyst. I'd fail if I tried, she said. Try what? asked her analyst. She didn't know. Her analyst let five minutes pass with the weight of silence pressing down on his chest and on Lyla's too. And then the session was over. Dr. Frankenstein at least had wires that connected to his monster.

Dr. Berman sat on her bed and spilled the entire contents of her jewelry box out on the spread. She placed the pieces in order. There was a line of bracelets, three Tiffany's silver bangles and the gold one with a small diamond and a small ruby linked one to the other by a row of emerald stars, from her husband on their twentieth anniversary. It was engraved with their names on the inside. Sometimes she thought when she placed it on her wrist before one formal dinner or another she thought it looked more like a handcuff than a piece of valuable metal. There was the necklace Betty had given her: the one that Justine had surely stolen. She should return it but how could she without violating patient confidentiality. On the left side she placed necklaces of various kinds of precious stones and pearls that had been formed in the depths of coral reefs across the datelines and as far from Central Park West as the imagination can go. On the right there were earrings, not so small and delicate, not so discreet in their value. Above, set in the tufts of the velvet was a ring with a ruby stone the size of her thumbnail and a gold star with a chain that she had never worn. Why was it there? Once they had gone to a meeting in Israel. Was the chain a worthless souvenir, a giveaway from some pharmaceutical company, or had she wanted it, purchased it from some shop in the lobby of the King David Hotel? The real diamond necklace her husband had given her when they married was in a safe in a bank vault. The name of the bank was emblazoned on the cover of her checkbook so it would never be forgotten. The diamonds themselves, having been taken from a mine in Africa, carrying with them the memory of geologic ages and human bondage, saw no more light then they had back in the mine.

With determination, Dr. Berman took her date book and on one of the back pages she began to catalogue the baubles, the valuable baubles laid out before her. She wanted to write this down so she would be able to tell if someone stole from her. She wanted to write this down the way the mayor of Amsterdam might want to add another brick to the dike. It tired her. But she persisted. When the cleaning lady knocked on the door wanting to do her job, Dr. Berman screamed out, Go away. And then she scooped up all the jewelry and placed it back in the large heavy box and carried the box into her bathroom, her beautiful beige marble bathroom, and she locked the door and sat on the floor, unwilling to come out, until late in the evening. What were they these jewels? She could throw them all away and nothing in her life would change.

She canceled her supervision appointment with the young analyst, the third week in a row that she had canceled.

Lyla's analyst was going away to a conference on "Object Relations in Early Childhood." He didn't tell her that he told her he would be out of his office for the week of the fifteenth to twenty-second. Object relations is the technical term for the fact that human beings need someone to care for them and someone to care for and if they don't have an object relation they die, literally sometimes, if they are babies, almost always, in spirit. Object relations is a phrase invented to convince analysts that they were talking about something you could put under a microscope, like dividing amoebas or RNA loops or enzyme production in the female frog. It also served to dignify the real story: who loved me, who loves me, who loved me not, who loves me not. The old daisy petal pull of childhood which is after all the main and maybe only drama, unless you are a Yankees fan or a collector of rare stamps, both of which serve as ways to evade the real question: who loves me, who loves me not.

The young analyst's brother had said to him, What's the matter with you analysts? You make the Politburo look like a town meeting in Akron, Ohio.

Conflict can be a sign of vitality, the young analyst had answered. Agreement is the sign of a fascist organization.

And this penis envy stuff, said his brother. For God's sake, you can't believe that.

The young analyst shrugged. He'd read all the articles. He knew all about Freud and Anna O. and the unfortunate judgments made along the way.

My brother is not my friend, he said to Dr. H. just before his session ended.

Very unusual, said his analyst.

There had been major wars inside psychoanalytic institutes. The young analyst knew all about them. There was Freud and Jung who parted company over questions of a religious sort. If you looked at their quarrel from a great enough distance you would see two giant behemoths with tusks at the ready pawing at the ground, ready to fight for dominance of the wild lands that reached north and southwest and east as far as the eye could see. There was Ferenczi, the Hungarian who wanted to put his patients on his lap when Freud wanted them untouched on the couch. Then there was Melanie Klein and Anna and the question of just how murderous was the infant mind. While sleeping peacefully in its basinet was the baby in fact chopping up parts of parents and sending death signals to invisible predators? Did children wish to devour their mothers and if so should you reveal that fact to them or not? That disagreement almost undid the London institute and made the New York ones tremble.

No one threw anything at Donald Winnicott when he came to America expressing a Kleinian idea or two but they did make him miserable with their derision and the night after his lecture he died of a heart attack. These New York psychoanalysts played for real. They didn't have disagreements on the nature of the human mind, they had territories to defend, borders that could not be crossed without proper passports. They played for keeps. And keeps was a trench in which many bodies were buried. Psychoanalysis was a science indulging in mayhem. Like priests fornicating in the parish house, this was to be expected. Freud believed he was a scientist. He had no interest in becoming a rabbi leading his followers into paradise with enchanting song and dance. And he was not a peaceful man, serene in his convictions. He thrived on the rivalry and the combat among his followers. He had favorites and non-favorites and the intrigues were political, tinged with sexual flirtations, and always mattered. After all the stakes were high. Was there a dangerous core of the human mind that expressed itself in dreams and went about disguised as politics or art or business the rest of the time, or wasn't there?

The young analyst had many questions about this or that part of the theory or that but he did believe unconditionally that the underground rivers of the unconscious existed in real time and crocodiles lined their banks.

The conference was in New Hampshire but the young analyst did not tell Lyla where he was going or why. Perhaps her guesses would open a path, would let him see her connection to him. Maybe she won't really care, he said to his own analyst.

Why would you think that? Dr. H. asked him.

The conference was only a four-day matter but the young analyst took an extra two days to visit his old roommate in Boston and to attend a Red Sox–Yankees game, which was lost by New York in the final inning, leaving a disgruntled young analyst with an urge for pot, a memory of a smell that filled his dorm room, carrying with it both defiance and peace.

And during this vacation, this brief suspension of her treatment, Lyla wilted. Like a plant without water she seemed to contract. She had bad dreams that woke her at night. She called her mother even more often and she thought more seriously about going home, although it wasn't actually her old home. I may visit, she said to her mother, who said, Yes, come, come as soon as you can. Lyla went online to look for airfares and direct flights. But she made no reservations.

When the following Monday her sessions resumed she arrived at the office looking unkempt, a kind of unemployed look, a rejected wife look, a who-cares-if-my-skirt-is-on-backwards look. Her analyst wondered if she had showered in all the time he had been away.

She had nothing to say to him. She stared at the ceiling as if a message from God had appeared in the faded yellow paint. Are you upset at our missed sessions? said the analyst after a very long time. No, said Lyla. I don't need you. I don't even like you. I avoid men with weak chins like yours. I am not going to keep on seeing you. I'm through.

Because I went away for a week? he asked. You're angry, he observed.

And Lyla did not weep. She said, I hate you. She said it coldly. She said it like a knife was placed between her teeth. She said it for eternity, for all of time. Her analyst waited.

What are you thinking? he finally said.

Nothing, she said, but in her rose a new unexpected feeling. As if she weren't a young woman whose husband had just left her for—for a man—but as if she were a terrible beast of the darkest forest, with a bloodlust for all living creatures, a desire to gnaw and smash and violate and trample and tear apart and spill to the ground the tissue and the muscle of other creatures, as if nothing but her great roar of rage existed and she would devour everything in front of her, wearing only her Nike sneakers, her red sweater, and the Banana Republic skirt she had on backwards.

She became very pale. She thought she might faint. I guess I'm not made of sugar and spice, she said.

I admit to a few puppy dog tails myself, said her analyst.

That night the analyst said to his wife, Do I have a weak chin?

I think you're perfect, she said to him, although of course she didn't.

Then in the real world something happened.

There was a black mole on Lyla's inner thigh. She ignored it. Two months later she had a dream about a mountain that kept sliding toward her. She mentioned to the young analyst that this mole on her thigh looked like a tiny mountain. He suggested she go to the dermatologist. There was a wait in a small room.

There was a quick cut. She put Neosporin on the little wound. There was Lyla's belief that all would be well. She was young. Everything lay ahead of her. Everyone has moles, thought Lyla. I will be all right, thought Lyla.

But the doctor called and she wasn't all right. Melanoma, said the doctor. Are you sure? said Lyla. He was sure.

How does that make you feel? asked her analyst.

That is a really stupid question, she said.

It was, he agreed, clumsy and stupid. Why had he asked it?

Because he was nervous. Because he was scared for her but didn't want to say so. Because he always believed that the sky could fall down on your head at any moment. Because despite being a doctor, he was afraid of the void, the pain that could come before the void, and sickness of cells, nerves, sinews, brain stems, that kind of sickness, he was afraid of that too.

Chemo? asked Dr. Berman in a very girlish voice. She too was afraid of death. You can live a long time these days, she added. I know, said her supervisee.

Patients get sick and die. You need to get used to it. You're not Saint Teresa and you have no weapons to rescue the physical body. She said that coldly. As if he were a delinquent child.

The polish on her fingernails was fire engine red and chipped. Her hands repulsed him slightly. The young analyst repeated the conversation in his own session the next day.

Later that evening Dr. H. wondered if Dr. Berman was sick herself. How old was she exactly?

Lyla Shulman called her ex-husband. Do you want to meet me for a drink? he asked. No, she said.

She said to her analyst that she had dreamt about her mother.

In the dream she saw her as a shark swimming in a turquoise pool, circling and circling waiting for the menstrual blood of her daughter to draw her close for the final kill. This seemed something of an exaggeration. All her mother had actually done was ask her daughter to come home, so she could provide refuge for her child at a difficult moment in her life. To paint so dark a view of her mother was surprising, at least to Lyla.

The analyst said: It's your dream.

Lyla said, You probably made me dream it. The young analyst considered what a wonderful thing it would be if he could only put dreams into his patient's heads. It would speed things up. It would give him power, and he was not one to shun a little power. Lyla said, If you met my mother, you might like her.

Why? asked the analyst. And Lyla could not find one single reason. They had nothing in common. The analyst however heard in her remark the thunderous footsteps of old rivalries accompanying the insulted, the wounded, and the powerless into old age. Lyla Shulman knew, even if she did not admit it to her analyst, that there was in that description of the shark in the swimming pool, truth. The young analyst sneezed. He may have been allergic to the discontents of civilization.

She won't die, said the young analyst. Probably not, said Dr. Berman. But I suggest you inform the institute that you will need another patient to meet the supervision requirement anyway. A backup? asked the young analyst. Yes, said Dr. Berman. This one is going home to her mother.

One beautiful spring night when the dogs were out in the park with their owners and there was a concert on the Great Meadow so crowds of people with blankets and picnics carried in bags and baskets were moving along the paths, Dr. Z. said to Dr. H. as they pushed their way toward the East Side where their meeting was about to begin, In my dream last night I had a pack of cigarettes in my pocket and I slowly took one out and lit it and I inhaled.

Dr. H. said, And then?

Dr. Z. said, I woke up.

Dr. H. said, I remember cigarettes.

five

How much did the child know and when did she know it? Her mother would worry about that and even discussed it with her therapist, more than once. You think, Dr. Berman had said, you behaved selfishly, a remark that was intended to open a new road of inquiry but instead resulted in two missed sessions. The mother's sister was a patient of Dr. Z.'s, and so when certain nervous symptoms appeared in Portia's mother that had no physiological basis, Dr. Z. had recommended that she see Dr. Berman.

The child, Portia, had an imaginary family named Smullian. The name was chosen because it sounded like *million* and *billion* and *smudge*. A smudge was a black mark across a page, a smudge was dirt on your dress, a smudge made something perfect imperfect and Smullian was the right name for this family—a mother and a father and a boy child and a dog. The imaginary dog was always hungry and the others never remembered to fill his bowl. The father was a lumberjack in the forests way up north and they lived in a cabin in the woods. The mother was in the kitchen baking bread day after day. Sometimes she went for walks with the boy and the dog and they picked yellow flowers and filled vases with golden petals that floated into the child's hair. The father's ax was always within arm's reach even when he was watching television and he took it into the shower with him. He said that an ax was a dangerous tool and should never be left unguarded.

Yes, Portia was a daydreamer. It was not bad to be a daydreamer. Her mother had said you could grow up to be a screenwriter or a test pilot. Her father was a rising financial officer of a prominent real estate firm. Her mother was the CEO of an organization that raised money for medical supplies for distant African nations. Portia could find those nations on a map; recite their names in alphabetical order. Portia knew that many children were not able to get the vaccinations her doctor had given her. She understood how fortunate she was in the accidental geography of her birth.

The Smullians lived in a cottage in the woods. Portia and her parents lived in an apartment on West Seventy-second that had once been half of the parlor floor of a robber baron's winter home.

Portia had outgrown her princess dresses. They lay crumpled in a box in the back of her closet, the tulle, the rhinestones, the petticoats, the lace straps, ignored. She was allowed one half hour of video games a day and another half hour of Nickelodeon. She sometimes watched *The Wizard of Oz* or an old Lassie movie with her babysitter who picked her up at school, who stayed when her parents went out in the evening, who belonged to a Hindu temple in Queens where some weekends she would take Portia to be blessed by the large person who sat on a cushion in bright robes and touched Portia's head with his brown hand.

She had piano lessons on Thursday afternoons and an art class at the Museum of Modern Art on Saturday mornings and she had gymnastics on Wednesday after school and on Tuesday evenings the tutor came to prepare her for the tests for a different school, tests that she would soon be taking. Also she never had diarrhea, except once after dinner at a Thai restaurant near her father's office. She was the only one of her classmates who knew that diarrhea could kill you. Her life was full, rich with events, free from fear of kidnapping, bombing, earthquake, flood, avalanche, or volcanic eruption.

The Smullians however were not so lucky. There were wild beasts in their forest. The little boy had been bitten by a snake and would have died had his mother not sucked the snake's venom from his foot. A vicious wolf had leapt at his father's face and a thick red scar ran from the corner of his left eye down to his jaw.

The Smullian mother had bad dreams. Sometimes she woke at night and her hands were shaking. Portia would tell her it was just a dream, don't be worried, but the Smullian mother could not be comforted and she would sit by the window of their cabin and wait for dawn. She was afraid that if she fell back asleep she would have another dream, perhaps worse than the first.

The Smullian boy wet his bed which made his father very angry and once he slapped him in the face so hard that the child hid from his father and would not let himself be kissed, not ever again, not by that father.

Portia overheard her babysitter telling her friend Lola's babysitter that Portia's mother was so beautiful she might have been a movie star. Not that one, she had added, tipping her head toward where Portia stood a distance away, not far enough away.

The Smullian mother developed a rash, ugly red hives

appeared on her face and neck. The boy brought his mother a plant he had found under an oak tree. She rubbed the leaves on her face in hopes of a cure but the leaves only irritated the sores and more appeared.

Portia's mother went on a trip to Uganda with some benefactors on her board. She was gone three weeks.

During those three weeks Portia's mother experienced the vertigo of those who travel extensively around the globe. When she looked down from her airplane height she saw that her husband was small and insignificant and that the turning planet would soon toss them all into oblivion and this made her sad, especially sad for Portia who would also age and disappear. On the fifth day of the trip she accepted the key pressed into her hand by a member of her board who supported jazz concerts as well as a small experimental theater and had paid for an entire new gymnasium for his old and not financially struggling prep school in Massachusetts.

Was it love or curiosity? It was love she believed. Maybe it was just sexual pleasure. Her body responded to these new limbs as if doors had flung open, trumpets had played, and all through the following long days, discussions of budgets, meetings with project managers, approving or disapproving of fund-raising mailings, she could conjure up sensations that made her workday pass quickly and her dinners at home with her husband and Portia seem like long cruises with unpromising strangers. All this she told Dr. Berman.

Dr. Berman believed in Eros, in the goodness of libido. She considered her patient's new affair a sign of awakening, a start down a potentially dangerous path, but overall a sign of life, a stretching upwards. She had no disapproving words. She wasn't a priest. This was itself a kind of permission. Her patient's nervous stomach behaved better.

Portia was born red all over with a crust of something in her eyes. She was perfect and both parents felt instant love and gratitude so vast it could never be repaid.

Which is why you might have thought that Portia's mother would not have accepted that key. It was a dangerous act. She was risking all and that itself may have explained the way she tightly held the key in the palm of her hand and carefully put it in the inner pocket of her bag next to her passport home.

The Smullian mother was carried off to the nearest hospital hours away on a rough road in the back of the family truck. The Smullian father kept telling the Smullian boy not to worry, the doctors would save his mother. The Smullian boy could not imagine the death of his mother. He was brave and said nothing but he prayed nevertheless to the gods, to the stars, to the spirits of the earth and the sky. He promised he would never harm any creature on earth if his mother was saved. And in the hospital he waited in the emergency room and told no one he was hungry or thirsty and at last fell asleep on a couch. And he did not dream. His head was empty.

Portia noticed that the Smullian cabin had a water stain on the wall behind the parents' bed. There must be a leak she thought, when wild storms pass the rainwater must pound against the wall and seep into the cracks. It rained in the forest every night for hours and Portia could hear the sound of water running down a drain. She could see the dirt darkening around the tree stump at the corner of the yard and she heard the beating of pine needles dashing against each other, against the branches swaying with currents. The Smullian father told the boy not to worry. They were safe in the cabin. Portia worried anyway. She saw jagged flashes of lightning as the crashing thunder came closer and closer and then receded over the mountains.

The Smullian mother returned from the hospital. Her rash was much better. It had left her face and there were only a few marks on her forearms. She threw her arms around the boy and she pressed her body into her husband's and she said she would make chocolate cupcakes. Portia watched as the boy licked the bowl. But in the forest a jackal let out a scream, a hunger scream, and his prey tried to hide behind a rock, but the jackal was fast, his nails clicked on the stone as he jumped.

Portia's mother had a good trip. It had been long but worthwhile. She brought Portia a doll from a market near the AIDS clinic she was visiting. The doll had glass beads around her neck and a red dress. On her feet she wore tiny stitched sandals. Portia was not very interested in dolls but she was glad her mother had come back. It was expected that she would return but Portia had not entirely expected it.

What a beautiful doll, said her nanny. I'll give it to you, said Portia. Oh no, said the nanny, your mother brought her for you. Portia said nothing. Nobody can make you love something you don't love. Even a child knows that.

August, Portia and her mother and father went for a vacation on Cape Cod. Portia and her parents rented a cottage furnished with wicker chairs and Hopper reproductions and little light-houses rested on bookshelves. Portia's mother spent many hours of the day on her cell phone talking with her office. Portia's father took picnic baskets to the lake and Portia went into the water. She would not put her head under the water. She would not lift her feet from the stony bottom. Somewhere there was a snapping turtle in the lake and Portia watched for him, prepared for retreat to the shore if he approached.

One day the incoming fog slowly crossed the lake. There was no exact moment when the temperature dropped but in slow motion the gray seeped up the blue and the white clouds disappeared and deeper, wider dark ones spread over the nearby moored sailboats, over the weathered docks, over the children building a fortress, but then it was there, a drop in temperature, a quick folding of umbrellas, a packing away of the just unpacked sandwiches, the beach ball fetched quickly from the bushes.

Portia was there with her father and her father's colleague whose family had rented a nearby cottage and the two men had been talking about a third who had broken a promise. And then Portia's father said, I find vacations boring. His friend said, The weather's changed, let's go back to the cottage and watch the Yankees game. Portia said, I want to stay here. No, said her father. No one stays on the beach in the rain. I like rain, said Portia. I don't, said her father.

There were rules of course that should be obeyed. There were promises that ought to be kept. Portia's mother was aware of her obligations to her husband, to her daughter, to her own honor. She had never been a religious sort of person. But the Ten Commandments had long ago settled into her neurons and her blazing synapses and could not be easily erased. She was a decent person, considerate of those who worked for her, smiled at the doormen in her apartment building, caring about her friends, and above all proud of her family. Now there was this new man and this excitement in her body that would not go away, that made her nights sleepless, that filled her with dread just as it delivered shivers of joy, joy that she had almost forgotten was possible. However, as it was the world over, since *Homo sapiens* had straightened their shoulders and shortened their jaws and lived in groups that gathered and hunted and increased the tribe, some order had to be maintained.

Portia's mother did not believe in sin but she did believe in respect, in nursing the flame of love for one's mate even when that flame was flickering and threatening to leave her in the dark. But she simply couldn't stop, stop the meetings in hotel rooms at the end of afternoons, at lunches in out-of-the-way Italian restaurants that were no longer fashionable if they had ever been.

Portia's mother stayed later and later at the office. Portia's father spent more time at the gym and Portia herself spent more time with the Smullians. The boy Smullian hid his father's ax in the forest behind a large mossy rock. The father Smullian said that the forest was becoming home to thieves and he wanted to move them all into town. The mother Smullian went looking for the ax and she found it. After that the ax was kept on a high shelf in the closet.

Portia's father taught her how to play chess. In the evenings sometimes he would sit with her and explain the moves, white and black. Portia would watch his hands, fingers drumming on the arm of his chair with his eyes focused on the board and at those times she wanted for nothing. Then he would turn on the evening news and sink into the couch. Portia saw that his eyes often closed as he watched. Sleep was suddenly elusive. He tried pills. They made him groggy. They stopped working after one or two nights. He tried hot milk and late night movies.

Portia's mother had not meant for this to happen. There is no question that she was as shocked as anyone else that a stranger had slipped into the small space that she had allowed between her and her husband. It's just a passing phase, her best friend told her. Ignore the signals your hormones are sending. They will go away in time. I don't want them to go away, said Portia's mother, who then was certain she would lose her lover if she didn't admit, acknowledge to the entire world what was the new truth of her life. She was not cruel. There was no pleasure in this. She wept for her husband and the way he turned his head to the wall and refused to look at her when she explained it to him, an accident, a matter of fate, of true love. Like a surgeon who cuts to heal, she told him the truth.

And he moved out and took Portia and her nanny with him. The Smullians came too.

Two nights a week Portia returned to her mother's apartment and her old bed and her old room. Her mother read to her at night. The man who was not her father told her how lovely she looked and he bought her a two-wheeled bicycle and promised to teach her how to ride it, and he played board games with her before bedtime. She called him Mark, but she never said his name out loud when she was at her father's house.

The Smullian boy wanted to go to a regular school. He decided to run away to a nearby city. He wasn't sure how to get there. Portia could direct him. Portia could lend him some money from her drawer. But she didn't. So, he just waited for something to change.

Portia knew that it was very important to learn how to wait. A child is so small, the tunnel so dark and long and the way so treacherous that a child is best protected by waiting, patiently, without noise, for a change that must come with time.

What the Smullian boy needed was a friend. Portia knew it. It was not right for a boy to live in a forest so far from all others. She wanted to invite him into her bedroom, both of her bedrooms, and have him become her brother. But Portia was a cautious child and she could see that having a brother might be a calamity. She might be banished herself to a distant forest and a passing wolf might devour her or perhaps she would just disappear from lack of being seen. If no one sees you, it occurred to Portia, your body might forget how to be visible.

And so her mother explained the facts of life to her. And she said, You will grow up and have children of your own. I must? asked Portia. You'll want to, said her mother. No, said Portia, I won't.

That night she decided she was too old for the Smullians. She planned an avalanche, a giant block of snow from the mountain above, and she watched as it came roaring down the mountain and fell on the Smullians' cabin where the three family members were sleeping. The dog was on the boy's bed. The mother's body was curled next to her husband's. There was a terrible groaning sound, the roof cracked open and tumbled down. The cabin walls collapsed inward. Bones broke. It was swift and deadly, this avalanche, and there were no survivors.

Not quite true. Under the boy's bed, there lived a city family, in two apartments, across town from each other. There was a girl who lived there too, sometimes in one apartment and sometimes in another.

That family, Portia's family, survived the avalanche.

Portia's mother told Dr. Berman that Portia was doing well. She had made a new friend at school. Who is Portia? Dr. Berman was not sure. Had her patient told her about Portia before? Portia was at school. She must be a child, not a pet. Children are resilient, said Dr. Berman. They have resources that would astonish you. Dr. Berman stood up and ended the session with her usual nod. When she rose, Portia's mother saw a white napkin stained with food that Dr. Berman had been sitting on. She also saw a crushed banana in the corner of the chair. Portia's mother didn't want to say anything, but she was puzzled. Had she interrupted Dr. Berman's lunch?

My early morning patient left his hat on the end of the couch. It was one of those gray fedora hats men used to wear before they didn't. I could hear him in the outer hall but I didn't rush after him. I was going to put the hat on my desk just as the bell rang and I went to open the door for my supervisee. I tossed the hat on my chair because I didn't want to open the door with a hat in my hand. I walked back to my office and the supervisee sat down in the chair and I sat down on my chair and I could feel it under me: my patient's crushed fedora. I just sat there, imagining the little feather in the band bending apart. The hat did not look so good after forty-five minutes under my bottom.

Dr. H. told this story to Dr. Z. as they were waiting for their wives to join them for a Chinese dinner before the theater.

Dr. Z. said, Were you coveting your patient's hat?

Dr. H. said, Or other parts.

Dr. Z., What parts?

Dr. H., The part that is going on vacation to the fjords next month.

six

His mother had died just weeks before his bar mitz-vah. All the pink ribbons in the world wouldn't have been able to save her. The color pink made him want to throw up. His younger brother had been in the room the moment she stopped breathing. He said the dying was all right. He didn't think it hurt her. Del had been waiting his turn to go to her. He had felt like punching something all morning. He had felt like punching his brother for days. When his father came to tell him he could go in and see her, he felt like punching his father, who in fact looked like someone had already punched him, his face was caved in, unshaved and there was spittle on his chin and his hair was uncombed and his eyes had this strange evasive look as if he were ashamed, as if he had been caught stealing.

Now it was two years later and Del had been expelled from the fine school he was attending in beautiful New England where in the fall the leaves turned golden and red, and blew to the ground in a rain of glory: a fact of nature pointed out in the school catalogue along with the college acceptance record of last year's graduating class.

He had to see the doctor or the school his father had found in the city wouldn't take him. He had no interest in seeing the doctor. He had an interest in going to the park and smoking pot with his friends. He had an interest in powders and pills that changed the way you saw the world, kept you awake, and made you think no harm could come your way. He also liked video games in which flares, bombs, assault weapons figured prominently. He did not like Ulysses or Hector or Ajax or Agamemnon, old and dead, they bored him. But it seemed useful for the moment to tell his doctor all about the war in Troy. His doctor listened.

When her colleague, Dr. H., mentioned that the patient she had referred to him seemed to be willing to talk about Troy for the next two thousand years, Dr. Berman said, Troy. Not worth the loss of life and treasure. An old story.

It is an old story, said Dr. H., whose own father had died in the Korean War just months before his birth.

If I were Penelope, she said, I would have married one of those suitors.

The wealthiest one, I assume, said her colleague.

Of course, said Dr. Berman. Was either of them joking?

First he stole *Time* from the table in the waiting room and tossed it in the trash can at the corner. Then when the doctor excused himself to answer a knock on the consulting room door in the middle of the session he stole a small Indian statue of Vishnu that was sitting on a shelf behind his chair. An arm or a leg bulged out of his backpack but Dr. H. was thinking he should have brought an umbrella to his office that morning and did not notice. Del sold the statue to an art dealer in the East Village and felt very American, an entrepreneur.

His doctor had suspicions, but no proof. His doctor missed his Vishnu. He had bought it in a dusty shop in London the summer he had gone to an international conference there. He was going to give it as a wedding present to his cousin's son but then decided to keep it instead. It wasn't particularly valuable. His attachment was simply sentimental. But sentiment has a value too.

What is it about the killing of Hector that you find so interesting? asked his doctor. His patient was silent. The doctor was silent.

His patient said, I'm going.

Why? asked the doctor. His patient got up and walked out and slammed the door behind him and did not return.

What do I do? asked his father.

Give him time, said the doctor.

Even Odysseus showed up eventually.

He had a shank of black hair that fell across his forehead. He was tall and thin, maybe scrawny would be the better word. He wore black leather bracelets on his wrists with protruding silver bullets warning the world to stay away. Girls in fact were attracted to him. The smell of danger, the indifferent way he noticed their breasts, their legs, and the cloud of nicotine that clung to his clothes. The heavy iron cross he wore around his neck. Was he Dracula or was he Dracula's next victim. It was hard to tell. Girls knew that under the dark glasses, behind the tense smile, a boy was waiting for someone to hold him close and chase away the monsters from the depths of the closet. Girls thought they could find him when he couldn't find himself.

It is in the nature of some boys to drive their cars into cement walls. It is the nature of some girls to ride ambulances to the scene of the accident.

No needles. He was afraid of needles. But other things were all right. At night in the park, with some guys from uptown, at a party on Park Avenue with a girl from his school, other things were all right, even comforting.

His father had a cousin who had gone to Israel and had founded a dot-com that provided information on insurance options. It sounded dull enough to be something you could do in New Jersey. Del packed a duffel and flew El Al. Why not? Why anything? As the plane lifted into the air leaving Kennedy Airport, he looked out the window and down to the harbor below and saw the Statue of Liberty, torch raised like a middle finger into the sky. Goodbye forever, he said to himself, and then wondered why he had said forever. His father had supplied him with only sufficient funds for a six-month stay and his return ticket was in his backpack stuffed behind his iPod and the pack of condoms his brother had given him as a going-away present.

The meeting was downtown in the Village where the head of the appointments committee lived in a brownstone with geranium pots in the windows and a collection of paintings that included a Larry Rivers and an early Magritte. Some analysts understood how to survive in a city of rabid dogs and others became like mendicant priests, resisting investment tips from patients because of an ethical code, using up inheritances, sending too many children to schools that paused in their pleas for donations only on the Fourth of July when most of their marks were out of town.

In the cab on the way, Dr. Berman said to Dr. Z., Who would you be, if you had to be one character in the *Odyssey*? He thought: Agamemnon. It took him a half second to realize why. His wife, ten years ago, had left him for six months to move in with a TV producer. She came back. His late night committee meetings, the paper he was writing and rewriting, "The Narcissistic Cathexis to the Missing Object," had left her feeling abandoned. Or he just wasn't as good as the other guy in bed. She hadn't murdered him, but he was sure she wanted to. He said to Dr. Berman, I would be the horse.

You are not taking me seriously, she said. He was. An army of invisible fighters armed with steel blades sat within him, waiting for a signal that never came.

You would be Helen, Dr. Z. said to her as the cab moved slowly down Seventh Avenue. No, she snapped at him. Why be mortal when you can be a goddess, Hera, Venus, power to force others to bend to your will . . . He was silent. Personally he would prefer to be mortal. He did not think that eternal life was necessarily a good thing. Enough was enough.

So Del arrived at Tel Aviv airport. He waited in a long and interminable line for his passport to be stamped behind five children, two aunts, one grandmother, four great-uncles, father, mother, all members of a Hasidic family carrying a new TV, a printer, an air conditioner, and a small fridge, two Cuisinarts, ice cream makers, a laptop, a fax machine, a vacuum cleaner, in boxes, presents for relatives, or perhaps they were opening a store.

His cousin was waiting for him on the Israeli side of the fence and he was holding a sign high with Del's name written in block letters. Before the day was over Del was enrolled in a Hebrew-language immersion school in Jerusalem, settled in a dormitory room, and had found out where to buy cigarettes and how to stay away from the tourists who wandered around wondering why they felt like strangers on Ben Yehuda Street and at home in their place of exile, perhaps Scarsdale or Port Jefferson or Des Moines.

Well, said Dr. H. when he heard the news from Del's father. It doesn't surprise me.

It surprises me, said his father. I sent him to Israel, not to the twelfth century. Dr. H. said, This might be for the best.

It is not for the best, said Del's father. I don't want him to be one of those parasites who live off the work of others.

I'm sure, said Dr. H., that is not how he sees it.

Would you be pleased if he were your son? asked Del's father. Dr. H. didn't answer. Actually, he would be angry and hurt and sad and he would spend pointless time trying to figure out where he had failed his son. On the other hand, officially, theoretically, he believed in the variety of human possibility. He believed in resilience and solutions to grief that were not his own solutions. He believed, especially for this other man's child, that the choice belonged to Del and perhaps it actually was all for the best. At the same time he knew it was all for the worst, the very worst. If a person were to spend their lives on texts, he would prefer Shakespeare, García Márquez, the United States Constitution, the poetry of Dylan Thomas, anything that didn't require a costume from the winter season in Poland's backwaters, fresh made by the tailors of a long gone century not known for its logic. Del would have a coat of one color soaked in the primitive fears of the powerless and the poor.

I failed my son, Del's father told Dr. H. Dr. H. looked at the digital clock discreetly sitting on the bookshelf behind the man in the chair in front of him. He said, Every father fails their son: it started with Abraham and Isaac and I think it's fair to include God and Jesus.

Del's father was not amused. He did tell Dr. H. that his other son was pre-med at Princeton and that he himself had married again. His new wife, his second wife, his much younger wife, had given birth to a baby girl.

Congratulations, said Dr. H.

And so it was that Del, now named Avram in a round black hat, with a matching black beard, with a very white shirt, with strings hanging out beneath his jacket, met his father at the same airport where he had arrived just a few years before.

On the evening of the second day of his visit, Del took his father to the home of his rabbi, his teacher. He said to his father, This is a holy man, this is a good man. I am his student. Please understand. I want you to understand.

Del's father heard the urgency in his son's voice. Beneath the beard, he recognized his fiery child. I will try, he said. I promise you, I will try. Either way, he said, you are my son. He thought about embracing him, but the young man backed away. Not yet, the father thought to himself.

And all went well through dinner. The rabbi's wife served a pale plucked chicken and some stewed fruit. There were prayers before eating and even longer prayers after eating and the Jerusalem heat poured into the small apartment, and when the meal was over the rabbi said to Del's father, Your son has a gift. For what? wondered the father, but said nothing. He has a loving nature, said the rabbi. Really, said Del's father. He had not seen that in his son.

Del's father looked at his son. Your brother misses you, he said. Write him a letter at least.

Avram shook his head. No, he said. This is my family now.

I don't understand, Del's father said to the rabbi, I thought you people had a commandment about honoring fathers and mothers.

We do, said the rabbi.

Del's father said to his son, You weren't meant to take that bar mitzvah as a draft notice.

Del (Avram) said, I have a people, a faith, a place. You have nothing.

Del's father did not feel love for his son. He swept the bread crumbs that had gathered at his place at the table into a small mound. He felt contempt. He also had stomach cramps. There had once been a little boy in his wife's lap, his head leaning on her breast, and his wife had been reading. And the wild things said we love you so we could eat you up, and the child had said, again, he wanted to hear it again, and the father had hopes, and those hopes he no longer had.

But he had something. It just wasn't something that could be put into a slogan, into a sentence. He could eat a meal without declaring allegiance to anything. It was his life and it had meaning even if he believed it had no meaning which is what, philosophically speaking, he believed.

Del's father who was now the father of a third-year medical student intending to specialize in neurology, an older son who was planning to move to a small settlement on a hill west of Nablus, and he was the father of a little girl who lived on the Upper West Side of Manhattan and wore princess masks at Halloween, a sight that her father had actually found frightening. He had trouble sleeping. He had become irrationally afraid of losing his mind. His wife had begged him to see someone.

Del's father told Dr. H. that he would not be allowed to meet or even see from a distance the grandchild that had just been born in Israel to his son and his wife. The reason—and here Del's father turned pale and his glasses misted over, and he took a long time before he was composed enough to speak.

Del, now named Avram, says that the secular Jews, Jews without synagogues, Jews in modern suits, Jews who ate bacon with their scrambled eggs, Jews who worshiped the false idols of science and fell to the temptations of the theater and the opera, in Europe in the first half of the twentieth century, caused the Holocaust.

Dr. H. said, Bullshit.

Del thinks, his rabbi thinks, they all think, that the Jews who did not keep kosher, did not keep the Sabbath holy, who did not follow the laws made God so angry that he brought down on their heads the catastrophe. He did it in the days of the Babylonian Exile. The prophets warned the Jews to behave in a way more pleasing to God and they ignored the prophets and first the Assyrians and then the Babylonians came down the mountain pass and swept them off to exile. It was the Jews' fault for straying. That's what they believe.

Bullshit, said Dr. H. again.

My son believes, Del's father said, there is a straight line from Sigmund Freud's Christmas tree to Auschwitz. That is what my son believes and he is afraid I will corrupt his child with the leprosy of the modern world. My son believes that the way I live caused the death of six million souls. What kind of a God would do that, would punish like that? asked Del's father. How could a sane person believe that? he asked.

Dr. H. thought: Sane people believe that God gave his son to the ordeal of crucifixion for the salvation of mankind. They believe that a baby can be born without a human father and that angels are singing in heaven above and that we are more than flesh and bone and will live in the clouds forever. Sane people are no test of sanity.

Del's father said, My son despises me.

The trains had moved across the continent under the usual constellations that revealed no heavenly secrets. The trains had been packed with disappointments, debts, plans, affections, sores, hunger pangs, soiled clothes, imperfect loves, sexual dreams, memories of music, math, misdeeds, cruelties large and small traveling all night with them to the chambers where the gas blew from spigots in the ceilings and God had not stopped them and it is reasonable to wonder why not and to find a reason that spares God from judgment (if it is not his fault it must be ours) and keeps his presence among the Jews, sacred and central so that chaos is banished and order restored.

God did not disappear in the Shoah. He was punishing his errant people. The rabbi explained this to Del's father. And Del's father did not accept the explanation. His voice had almost failed him. It came out thin and whiny. He had said to the rabbi, little children, babies, people who had harmed no one, Your God did this?

Dr. Berman had a dream that she told no one. In it Paris appeared with a golden apple and he gave it to her. She was walking in Central Park and she was wearing her black suit with a Hermès scarf and the gold pin that sat like a fist on her lapel. Paris said to her, You are the woman I have been waiting for. And she said to him, in her dream, I know. When she woke she remembered her dream. That morning when she looked in the mirror she saw the marks of age, the slip of skin, the drape of chin, the loss of rose and dew, and she saw the tight pull at the edges of her mouth where the lust of her youth had drained away. She considered that in her dream Paris might have been standing in for her plastic surgeon.

Dr. H. said, So the Holocaust is your fault. Perhaps you caused the genocide in Cambodia or the droughts in Africa. Those little children in Mali with big eyes and round bellies dying in refugee camps, you must have done it. Maybe it was that last ham sandwich you had.

Del's father felt irritated. I'm serious. That rabbi really believes that.

You must be angry, said Dr. H.

At least your son has a family, said Dr. H.

Not mine, said Del's father, who was also Avram's father whether he liked it or not.

I could kill him, said Del's father.

We'll talk about that, said Dr. H.

And they did.

Dr. H. said to Dr. Z., I can't believe I said bullshit twice in a session today.

Was it bullshit? asked Dr. Z.

Yes, said Dr. H.

No harm done then, said Dr. Z.

seven

Dr. Z. said to his patient Ruth Glassberg, who was sitting opposite him white faced cracking her knuckles one after another, I understand.

No you don't, said his patient, in a whisper. He waited. I feel so ashamed, she said. I can't tell anybody.

You'll have to tell Will, he said.

I sent him an email, she said. He hasn't called. He's probably been in meetings all morning.

Do you believe your daughter has become less of a gift to you and Will since you opened the mail at 9:30?

Of course not, said his patient.

Do you find her less worthy today than yesterday? he added.

Of course not, but—, and the tears began again. I'll have to tell my sister. She'll ask. She knows the letter came this morning. She had one of the partners in her firm write a letter for us. She said he had given so much at the benefit auction we were certain to be accepted.

Dr. Z. said, In this matter there are no certainties.

Planes fall from the skies. Tornados sweep across counties tearing down walls and crashing into bridges. Tsunamis come out of the ocean and little children who have not received spectacular scores on their ERBs are drowned among the debris of floating beach chairs.

Dr. Z. did his residency on the pediatric cancer ward of Sloan Kettering. Dr. Z.'s mother had survived the war as a refugee in Singapore and had never gone to kindergarten. She was literate in three languages nevertheless.

You don't understand, said his patient again. I feel judged. I feel as if everyone is pointing at me. She's not smart enough or maybe the damned nursery school wrote a better recommendation for that fat little girl, Clare Lang, who practices the piano two hours every day. It's not fair.

Dr. Z. sighed. It wasn't fair. His patient's daughter was surely as lovely and as reading-ready as the little girl whose mother was right now rejoicing and calling every distant relative she could think of to report her success.

I feel, said his patient, as if my daughter is damaged, tarnished, and less graced by fortune than she was before. Now there will always be a beforehand and an after. Her birthday party is next week. How can I have a birthday party?

Dr. Z. had an impulse that was unworthy of his training, his discipline. He suppressed it. Instead he said, One day you'll laugh about this little letter from the world-famous school that can read the future no better than the average fortune-teller at the county fair. The place your child will one day take or the college she may attend or the man she will love or the work she will do or the children of her own she will have are not changed because of this admissions director you tell me is so famous, or her cracked crystal ball. What old wound has this opened?

His patient sat still.

I don't know, she said.

I have a headache, she added.

I have no doubt, said Dr. Z.

He had one too.

Have you ever seen a patient with hysterical paralysis? asked Dr. H.

No, said Dr. Z. Vienna had dozens of patients who went blind or deaf or couldn't walk, because of buried thoughts they couldn't think. It doesn't happen now. Not in New York City.

It would be better if it did, said Dr. H.

Everyone is on to the game, said Dr. Z. Our patients know enough about the unconscious to be almost always conscious. We've lost the power of the surprise. They read Freud in high school. They don't hide away memories in a deep vault. They tweet them. So they go on walking and seeing but remain miserable.

And not so easy to help, said Dr. Z.

We do have pharmaceuticals, said Dr. H.

Thank God, said Dr. Z.

If only they worked better, said Dr. H.

If only, said Dr. Z.

Narcissism, said Dr. H.

Borderline personality disorder, said Dr. Z.

Bipolar depression, said Dr. H.

Wonder what Freud would have made of LSD? said Dr. Z.

Blown his brains out, I'm sure, said Dr. H.

Leaving Dr. Z.'s office, his patient walked along Amsterdam Avenue. She saw the latest fashions, the sweaters that hung to the knees, the leathers with fur collars tempting in the small store windows, but her attention was elsewhere. There was just one other school to hear from, by the end of the week she would know if her daughter could compete with everyone else or had been exiled. Exiled to what? She felt transparent, as if the people walking past her could tell that she was injured.

That wasn't a new feeling.

It didn't arise because of the school letter. She often felt that her clothes were wrong. Her opinion on the issues of the day wanting. She often suspected that she was a lacking a dimension. For no reason at all she felt afraid, afraid that she was less, lesser, least. In whose eyes? In her own eyes, Dr. Z. had said. There were millions of souls in the city, all kinds and colors and shapes, but sometimes she believed that if she vanished the tabloids wouldn't scream out her disappearance in bold type and someone else would take her place in her bed and Will might not notice and only her daughter, the rejection letter daughter, would ask about her for a month or so.

A woman ahead of her stood at the crossing waiting for the light to change. There were no cars coming. Move, thought Dr. Z.'s patient. And then she had a vision, a dream fragment that broke through the barrier of reason into the daylight. In her vision she pushed the woman at the curb with all her strength, just as a car turned the corner, and the woman was tossed in the air and her scream rolled along Amsterdam, past the Tasti D-lite, past the vegan pizza restaurant, past the jewelry store with the little gold and turquoise earrings in the window, and everyone stood still and stared.

She would never push anyone into the street.

She told herself, as her beating heart slowly returned to its normal rhythm, that she would tell Dr. Z. about this waking dream. It wasn't so bad to think of harming someone as long as you didn't do it and she would never.

Then as the light changed it came to her that someone else might have the same thought, someone right at that moment might be thinking of pushing her into the street. She looked over her shoulder. An old man, using a cane, was right there. What was he thinking?

Was it the interview? Had Laura been too quiet? Had she not wanted to draw a picture, had she remembered to use many colors? Had she sucked her thumb? She knew better than to do that but maybe if she was scared or feeling shy . . . but should a child be banned from a school for acting like a child? Had that prissy retarded teacher who thought Laura wasn't getting enough sleep said that in her reference?

Shame embraced her. Shame filled every crevice of her mind. And fury. Her child, God how could anyone not see the wonder of her child, the sweet smell of her hair, the long lashes like her father's, the small perfect ears, how could anyone not see her beauty, outside, inside. It was, in some way that she couldn't have explained, her fault. Her failure, her shame, her shame alone.

Maybe it was because they weren't hedge fund people and would never be able to do much more than staff the bake sale. Maybe it was because she had not gone to an Ivy League college herself, but Will was a journalist. He was a journalist people talked about, wrote comments about online. Maybe it was because they weren't interesting enough, just white folks from Long Island. Some Indian computer genius's daughter, some British rock star, a Chinese diplomat's twins, a Bosnian Moslem with the World Bank, a black professor of economics, their children would have been given a place and Laura, Laura was rejected.

And Dr. Z.'s patient felt helpless to protect her daughter, to shield her from harm, to secure for her the best that life could bring. Her love for her child could not be contained in her breast. She ached with it. She limped forward with it. She leaned against the side of a building hoping the force of it would abate.

Hours later, after Laura had her bath, had watched her half hour of TV and had listened to *Bread and Jam for Frances* for the thousandth time and curled up under her quilt with her thumb in her mouth, her mother and father opened a good bottle of wine, as useful in bad times as good.

We could move to back to Great Neck, Will said.

Never, she said.

And with that word came the first call to battle. It was a firm call, a not-to-be-resisted call: Something, she would do something. There has to be an end to wilting and a beginning of blooming. She would bloom and so would Laura. That is what she would tell Dr. Z. She loved Will and Laura and Dr. Z. Not necessarily in that order.

The nuns were right, said Dr. Z., who wasn't Catholic and therefore had great affection for nuns. It is pride—vanity—that makes us suffer.

Dr. H. shook his head. It's fear of invisibility.

Dr. Z. said, You mean of someone else's invisibility, someone with a cloak draped over his head so his enemies cannot see him following them down a dark alley?

Dr. H. said, Not fear of the robber, creeper, strangler, but fear of not being seen. What, said Dr. H., would happen if the mother came to the crib to pick up the child after the nap and the child was invisible and she couldn't hear the cry and the child had lost its sinew, its substance, and was there, calling for help, but the mother couldn't see or touch the infant body. What then?

Dr. Z. said, Absurd.

Dr. H. said, Not so absurd.

Dr. Z. said, I wouldn't put that in print.

Dr. H. said, I won't.

Dr. Berman spoke with her usual authority. She seemed enveloped in a cloak of royalty. She never said maybe, or I don't know, or I wonder if. She spoke in the affirmative, or the negative, clearly. Which is why none of her colleagues at the wine and cheese gathering after the presentation by the London analyst (who was likely suffering from jet lag) mentioned to her that she had left her purse in the auditorium. A student retrieved it and presented it to her as if it had just slipped to the floor.

But in the taxi crosstown it was clear that her mood was dark.

Once, she said, when I began, we were gods in this city. Now they think we're clowns. No one, then, no matter their bank account, their name in the society pages, their awards or reserved places at restaurants, no one was as respected and feared as our small band.

Perhaps, said Dr. Z., that was not so good. We began to have delusions that we actually were mind readers, holy priests. I'm surprised no one ever suggested a balloon of Freud for the Thanksgiving Day parade. We lost perspective on ourselves.

Dr. H. agreed.

Dr. Z. went on. All that hallelujah faith in pharmacological cures or self-help books, and TV gurus, steals our thunder. We might as well have tanks of leeches in our offices. We could do acupuncture as a sideline. Or maybe we should illustrate our papers with gold vines on the sides of the page and small ink portraits of our offices nestled under giant capital letters. And then we could be humble friars and revered for our piety until a new renaissance restores us to our pedestals.

Dr. H. laughed. Dr. Z. was a large man with big hands that could never have wielded a tiny brush with a drop of gold paint on its tip. I'm not holding my breath, he said, a psychoanalytic renaissance is beyond imagining.

I can imagine it, said Dr. Z.

Dr. Berman said, I can't.

I can imagine what Frederick Crews, the anti-Freud superhero, would say about your wrapping yourself in a brown burlap gown stained with gold leaf drips, said Dr. H.

Our critics are gleeful that the science of psychoanalysis, like all the other sciences, commits errors. But we too learn from error, move forward and backwards, acknowledge wrong paths, try others. What did they expect from us? Chemistry was not flawless at the beginning. The elements were named earth, air, water, and fire: no one gave up on chemistry. You have to start somewhere. Dr. Z. sighed.

We still have patients, said Dr. H.

Some, said Dr. Z, and students, not the ones looking for a Nobel Prize, but students nevertheless.

Not so many, said Dr. Berman.

Enough, said Dr. H.

Enough for what? said Dr. Z.

Bring back the glory days, said Dr. Berman.

Dr. Z. said, Not likely.

Dr. H. said, Maybe.

Dr. Z. said, Uh-huh.

Good night, said Dr. Berman. They had arrived at her corner.

eight

The patient had said she was allergic to cats. So Dr. Berman had picked Lily up and brought her to the kitchen and told the housekeeper to keep her there. Lily, blue-gray with green eyes, with long silken fur, a languid walk and a manner of sleeping, constantly sleeping, that made it clear that her dreams were comfortably primal.

Also she was incapable of breaking confidentiality, so she could stretch out on the windowsill across from the couch and never blush, or wince or weep.

The patient had the two o'clock hour three times a week. Before the bell rang, Dr. Berman removed the blue velvet cushion she kept on the patient's chair. This patient required the entire space for her body. In fact it would be fair to say that the patient required an even wider chair than could be found in any showroom, any catalogue in the known universe.

The patient, Edith Forman, had been born with large bones and wide hands and feet and eyes the color of the Caribbean Sea at sunrise. She had tended toward plumpness as a child, a small tire of fat had encircled her midriff, but she was always in the middle of games, jump rope, tag, hide-and-seek and her smile was wide and winning even through the years when her teeth made appearances and disappearances, crashed into each other, and spread too far apart. Her father spoke of her as a beauty. Her mother brushed and braided her hair each morning before she left for work.

Edith had no explanation for it, the hunger that had come on her with her first period, the hunger that brought weight to her thighs and broadness to her waist, and ruined her face as her eyes seemed to shrink and her features thickened and coarsened. The first diet worked for a while but then it didn't. The diet camp for overweight teenagers brought about a miracle loss of twenty pounds regained before Halloween. It wasn't even hunger anymore that prompted Edith to store under her bed packages of cookies and boxes of chocolate candy shaped like the shells of the sea. Perhaps it had never been hunger, but rather an intolerable vacancy, an emergency of hollowness. Could the body confuse itself with a sinkhole in a desolate swamp?

She loved to cook, she appreciated the smells of warm butter, the different olive oils, the spices cardamom and cinnamon and garlic and pepper and the stirring and the boiling. She made meals for her friends but often was too embarrassed to join them as they ate. She would spoon a small portion onto her plate and then push it around from side to side. Later when she was cleaning up, later when the plates waited in the sink, she would scrape everything left over, bitten into, mashed, sliced, stained, into a bowl and eat it all, in happy privacy, in tormented gluttony, in fear of what monster lived within her and sometimes would not rest until she had eaten everything in the cabinet, and the refrigerator and the pistachio nuts she kept in a bin on a top shelf in the hall closet.

Sweating, panting, tearful, she would go to bed, her large form tossing and turning, her stomach stretched, her bowels tight, her shame covering her, inflaming the sores between her legs that came from the chafed flesh that surrounded her vagina.

She was not yet thirty although it would have been hard to tell her age. Why had this happened to her? Could she ever be different? Should she have an operation? Could a knot in her intestines bring her happiness? These were the questions she wanted to explore with Dr. Berman. She was afraid of dying on the operating table. It was a small statistical possibility but not one she had invented. She had a dream in which she lay stretched out on an operating table, her hair under a blue nylon cap, her mouth filled with tubes, her arms stuck with needles and the doctors around the table still as statues under the stark light above and there was no sound in the room, only the beginning of bacterial decay, an audible tinkling of many tiny mouths, a feast beginning for the creatures of the coffin, who were multiplying in her extended lifeless gut.

Dr. Berman herself thought she would rather be dead than look like Edith, than feel like Edith, but then she knew herself well, vanity was not one of her more attractive qualities and vanity had its own problems which should all be put aside to help Edith, but Dr. Berman knew the odds were not with her, and God, the girl was frightfully huge, like something from a fairy tale written by the Brothers Grimm centuries ago.

Maybe a small tilt of a dented molecule in a gene that should have stood upright next to its neighbors had fallen just a fraction away so that Edith's appetite lost its regulator and a hole was created in the DNA that would spoil the blue-green eyes, the brain that could remember whole stanzas of *Paradise Lost* and the large-boned feet that if not for that tilting gene might have danced in the arms of a beloved night after night.

Had biology done Edith dirt or was it the unintended harm that is passed on generation to generation, mothers that ignore a baby when it cries, fathers that do not admire the miracle of life they have created, nannies that do their jobs with their minds on the rent they owe or the men or children who claim their own right to comfort against the pains of the stomach or the ear or the fear of the dark.

Was she abused by a father or an uncle? Dr. Berman favored the abuse theory. She saw incest as the Jack who would, menacing clown face and all, jump up on his rusty coiled wire if you just keep winding the little arm on the side of his tin box long enough. More usually, incest was only a wish, a wish as common as dandruff and tooth decay. But in addition to a wish it was sometimes an act, committed in the dark, under the sheets, a violation of the natural order, a thumb in the eye of morality, a stone thrown at the dignity and grace of the human family.

But Edith kept insisting her father would never harm her. He was not as willing as she would have liked to play Monopoly with her on Saturday afternoons. He was attached to his golf bag as if it were a third arm. Fifteen-inch yellow lined pads often emerged from his briefcase and he shut his study door and no one was allowed to disturb him when he worked after dinner, but he didn't, and Dr. Berman probed very gently, never had, touched Edith, in a way a father shouldn't. Nor had anyone else.

Or so Edith insisted. Provisionally Dr. Berman had accepted that Edith was not violated literally. But then what?

Sooner or later Edith would be able to tell her. First would come trust, and then would come passion and Edith would grow afraid that Dr. Berman might disappear from her life and she needed Dr. Berman who had promised nothing but in the act of accepting her as a patient had promised everything. She required Dr. Berman to answer her bell and sit opposite her again and again: no, not an imaginary Dr. Berman but the real one in the chair opposite her. Only if she were there, could Edith speak whatever it was she needed to speak, when she was ready, if she could.

Edith had a high voice, girlish, lovely especially if you didn't look at her as she spoke. She was immaculately clean, her nails were bright red and perfectly oval and she smelled of pine soap and oil that you purchased in health food stores. She had trouble rising from her chair at the sessions' end and she would hang on to the arm for support and her knee joints, burdened by folds of fat, creaked and strained.

Dr. Berman thought about Edith's heart beating underneath the pounds of breast tissue, muscle, fat from the abdomen pushing upwards. She thought about how hard it would be to do an autopsy on Edith. She forced the image out of her mind because it made her anxious. Edith was dying. But so is everyone alive, she told herself, including me: a fact so unbelievable she didn't even try to believe it.

Edith's dreams were nightmares and they often took place in the belly of a whale. She had explained to Dr. Berman that she had seen *Pinocchio* at a friend's birthday party when she was just starting school. She would never tell a lie, she said. She was a child with perhaps an exaggerated sense of honor. Did you want to be a real boy? asked Dr. Berman, who knew the answer to her question.

No, said Edith, I wanted to be a whale. And then she sat there, glaring, her jaw that folded into her neck set in a rigid line.

Dr. Berman wished she liked Edith better. She wished she could find something in her that made her try harder, push further.

In her nightmares Edith was sometimes very small, so small she could disappear down the sink drain if she fell over the edge. In her nightmares Edith sometimes opened her legs and swarms of herring flowed out over her thighs.

Without herring, millions of herring, all the other fish in the sea would die, the food chain would be completely destroyed, Edith told that fact to Dr. Berman who had never liked herring, too salty.

Edith had a recipe she had invented herself for fettuccine and capers. She printed it out and gave it to Dr. Berman. Dr. Berman would only eat pasta on rare occasions and she never cooked herself.

Does she want me to get fat? thought Dr. Berman.

Narcissism, borderline personality disorder, bipolar disturbance, all these nasty conditions were possible in the matter of Edith, but none of them fit exactly. That was because the slippery soul was very good at evading the doctor's diagnostic kit. Dr. Berman considered that Edith suffered from several pathologies at once, like a patchwork quilt she had once had as a child, made up of all the fabrics of old discarded dresses.

And then she considered the Sleeping Beauty theory, the one she would never have presented to her students at the institute or mentioned to a colleague. Objective proof, scientific testing was impossible. No grant would be forthcoming to test this theory. Nevertheless Dr. Berman considered that the wicked fairy was the culprit. This was the wicked fairy that had not been invited to the christening party. What mother or father, king or queen would invite the dark fairy of the forest to celebrate their daughter's birth? But the uninvited, the shunned fairy came anyway and cursed the infant in its blanket and said that she would die when she was twenty-one, poisoned by a needle from a spindle. Sometimes Dr. Berman thought the only reasonable explanation for the grief before her was the dark fairy, who hadn't been invited because she was the dark fairy, who came anyway and cursed on and on until it was a wonder any infant was sheltered from her ire.

And when Edith couldn't sleep at night, when the last of the nature programs went off the air, when the lights in the buildings opposite her apartment were all dark and there were no sounds of cars on the avenue and only the changing red and green traffic lights promised the return of the world outside, Edith would often go to the window seat and sit there looking up into the sky, where she could catch the flash of a plane with its lights blinking in the darkness as it crossed the park headed for LaGuardia Airport or going the other way to places Edith would never go. She might write a few lines in her notebook . . . She would think of the passengers on those planes, sitting side by side, husbands, wives, children, heads resting on shoulders, knees touching, and the reality of her life, the singleness of it, would run through her, leaving her breathless, awake, and waves of anger would lap at the edge of her consciousness, and then recede.

Sometimes she sang out the window, show tunes, operetta, country music, her mood would change and she might fall asleep on her sofa. She imagined a man listening, a man who would fall in love with her voice, who would never see her, but long for her always: a man who spent his nights waiting for her to sing and his days waiting for night.

Edith wrote poetry. Edith read poetry. Those two acts do not always go together but in Edith they did. She had small black notebooks on her desk, poems titled and dated. She had a stack of books on a table that she reached for again and again. There was Sylvia Plath whom she admired for turning on the gas and not staying her hand. There was Emily Dickinson who knew everything that Edith knew and had not obscured the truth, and made out of defeat a victory no one could question.

There was Marianne Moore and Elizabeth Bishop. Eccentric ladies, ladies who loved women, ladies who knew what it was like to believe that the clock might be lying, and time standing still while they looked at their lovers sleeping beside them. There was *The Aeneid* and *The Iliad* and *The Faerie Queene* and *Leaves of Grass*, and when Edith's mind seem ready to fly apart she could recite to herself Coleridge's "In Xanadu did Kubla Khan a stately pleasure dome decree," or Gerard Manley Hopkins' "The Windhover," *I caught this morning morning's minion, kingdom of daylight's dauphin, dapple-dawn-drawn Falcon, in his riding . . .* Ezra Pound, *petals on a wet, black bough*, and the words would restore her, like ammonia on a handkerchief under the nose of a fainting girl.

There was H. D., who had a vision of cannons and soldiers and death that appeared in silhouette on her wall when she was living in Vienna while undergoing analysis with Freud. Her vision came before the war that came before the war that followed the war and caused everyone to believe that the Enlightenment was no more than one of Houdini's master illusions, a fraud in other words.

Edith wrote short poems, thin poems, graceful poems, airy poems, but they each contained a moment that trembled in the air the way a fallen leaf might shift in the currents of a brook. She copied the final versions of her poems into a small thin notebook with a glossy purple cover. There were three note-books now on her bookshelf. There was also a bin, a laundry bin, holding the many drafts of each poem. She kept the bin in a corner of her room and covered it with a shawl she had bought at a street fair.

The notebooks were numbered and ordered. She knew the contents of each. She kept them near her bed on her night table so she could read them before falling asleep but she didn't need to open her notebooks. She could and did recite all her poems to herself whenever she wanted.

The time came when she told Dr. Berman about the poems. This was her darkest or was it her brightest secret. Some patients revealed fantasies of being whipped or thoughts of murdering their siblings or fears of sexual inadequacy or reported cruel deeds done in childhood. Edith's revelation concerned her poetry, which unlike her physical self could be hidden, kept pri-vate, away from prying eyes, mocking eyes, unloving eyes.

Ah, thought Dr. Berman, now I have you.

She waited for Edith to offer her the poems, to ask her to read them, but Edith hesitated. No one had seen her undressed since she was a child. It was true Dr. Berman was a doctor but never-theless the poems were too personal, too secret, something she would never expose. She could not give them to Dr. Berman.

Dr. Z. said, as the two men sat in Starbucks before a lecture at their institute by a French analyst known for speaking very fast and lisping, I think I may need an audio aid for this one.

Dr. Z. said, Why did we come? I'd rather be home watching the Giants game.

Dr. H. said, I'd rather be fishing.

Dr. Z. said, At night?
Dr. H. said, That was a metaphor.
Dr. Z. said, We're like poets. We write for each other.
And posterity, said Dr. H.
And the tooth fairy, said Dr. Z.

And then she would give them to Dr. Berman. If Homer could be blind, then she could be fat. Edith thought it through. If she never let anyone see her poems no one would ever know how it was in her country: the land of those whose bodies had betrayed them, or was it better to say those who had betrayed their bodies. Also if no one ever read her poems and no one knew she even wrote them, then she would remain hidden and if she were hidden she would be alone forever and if she were alone, this lonely, days without end, she would extinguish herself the way you put out a candle with a quick rubbing of your thumb and forefinger, or a swift breath serving as the wind of God terminating the light, preventing morning from coming up over the horizon.

Rimbaud was bipolar.

Ezra Pound was manic.

Simone Weil was anorexic and masochistic.

Emily, well Emily was an isolate with interpersonal terrors and talked to God too often for her own good.

Dylan Thomas was alcoholic and depressed.

Robert Lowell was lucky they found lithium. It kept him out of the hospital.

John Berryman jumped off a bridge when depression put its arm around his neck.

Allen Ginsberg wrote to keep his mother's schizophrenia at

bay but he needed drugs to do it, as well as religious hypnosis, hocus-pocus, lotus positions, and chants.

Robert Frost was mean as a snake.

Ted Hughes was twice the husband of defeated wives.

Sylvia Plath put her head in the oven, while two little children slept in the next room.

Anne Sexton didn't make it. Her analyst failed her.

Edith was a fat poet: a very fat poet who was at the moment alive.

And then there was something else. Dr. Berman had sat opposite Edith quietly for many months. She had leaned forward to hear her when her voice had been almost inaudible. She had listened to her talk of diets and her shame at the gluttony she only partially disclosed. She had given Edith her full attention and as a result the predictable had happened. A small space had opened in Edith's mind where she sometimes thought of things to tell Dr. Berman. And in that small space something new was growing, was it a small bud, a small new tender shoot of affection: was the word for it *love* and what did that love contain? Edith didn't know but it brought her hope, this feeling, and it belonged to her and was the gift she wished to give to Dr. Berman and this new feeling made her bring her poems, in their three full small purple notebooks to her session, each time for two months, that was twenty sessions before she actually opened her bag and produced the notebooks, just seconds before her hour was up.

Dr. Berman was about as fond of poetry as the next person. She had taken a course on the Romantics in college, a change of pace from pre-med chemistry that had been welcome. She admired poets, and the idea of poetry, but she didn't have the patience to let the words wash across her brain and sink in here and there. She was basically attracted to facts. They were mysterious enough. But she understood that Edith was opening a door, a door Dr. Berman had every intention of walking through. She put the poems on her desk, on top of a paper, "The Defensive Position in Melanie Klein," that had been submitted to the *Psychoanalytic Quarterly* and was awaiting a positive or negative reaction. Dr. Berman had been selected by the editorial board as a reader whose opinion would be given great weight.

Edith's three notebooks were slim, as slim as Edith was not.

Over the weekend Dr. Berman went to dinner with a friend. She forgot the name of her friend's daughter. She forgot how old the child was and if she was married or not. It was possible to carry on a conversation about that daughter, picking up clues as she went along. The effort however tired her and she did not go to the movies with her friend as planned but instead went back to her apartment and directly to bed.

She admitted to herself that her mind was a blackboard on which the questions for the exam, an important exam, had been written but a hand with an eraser had appeared and wiped away the questions and all possibility of answering them before she had a chance to open the blue book in front of her.

Edith spent the weekend as she spent every weekend, watering her plants, ordering food online, boxes of food that would arrive in clear plastic wrap. She would also go to the grocery store, early in the morning before most people were about, and there she would purchase only healthy food, apples and whole grain cereals and skim milk and packages of low-calorie diet bars.

Later if the sun was drifting across Central Park and the day was warm enough Edith would sit on a bench in the park and watch the young mothers pushing their strollers. She would watch the tiny silver scooters, the bikes with training wheels, she would stare at the pockets in the back of the stroller, stuffed with sweaters, diapers, a book, a baby bottle, a bag of cookies. What kind of cookies? She would guess.

Sometimes while she watched she would see a flash of anger cross a mother's face. She would see the tired eyes, the limp hair, the signs of sorrow or exhaustion in the midst of joy. Edith appreciated those sightings. And sometimes a line of a poem would float into her mind. And she would repeat the line over and over again, shutting out all sounds around her, all sights. She believed that these inward journeys saved her life and were her life.

Sometimes sitting on a park bench noticing that passersby saw her size and looked away as if embarrassed she would get angry. It is not your park, she would think. Cancer cells are in your breasts, she would think, you will die, she would think, and I will live. And she thought worse things than that, things that included pulling of nails and shaving of heads and blinding of eyes. These were not nice thoughts but if she had told Dr. Berman about them, Dr. Berman would have said they were just thoughts.

And then she would get up and go back to her apartment and write down the line that had come to her in the park and maybe add another.

Dr. Z. said to his friend as they were waiting for an education committee meeting at their institute to begin, I should have been a GP in rural Nebraska.

Dr. H. said, I should have been a Scientologist.

You're in a bad mood, said Dr. Z.

Dr. H. said, I don't think Scientologists have as many evening meetings as we do.

Dr. Z. said, You could practice voodoo and you wouldn't have any meetings at all.

Dr. H. said, Scientologists get to climb to higher spheres.

Dr. Z. said, Psychoanalysts get to tumble into the abyss.

The doors to the meeting room opened, the chair of the committee walked in.

Tuesday morning: Edith had her usual 2 p.m. appointment to look forward to later in the day. She put on her best smock over her jeans, jeans she had bought online where no one would see her, or ask her size.

Tuesday morning: Before the sun rose, pink and hopeful, over the East Side, on the other side of the reservoir, before the joggers and the walkers had begun their exercise, Dr. Berman woke up and for a moment wasn't sure if she was traveling. Had she come to another city, was she in a hotel? Soon it came back to her, the way a room settles down after a dizzy spell. She went into her office and saw the clutter on her desk. The paper she should be reading and the three notebooks that contained Edith's poems. She had not read them.

Lily walked over the desk gingerly, looked for a place to curl up and finding none went over to the couch and sat on the patient's pillow, yellow eyes staring and blinking at nothing in particular.

Dr. Berman had her coffee cup in her hand. She wanted to put it down. There were too many papers on her desk. She was upset. It was too much to have to clean her own desk. She had hired people to keep order in her house and they were not doing their job. She had to do everything herself. Bitterness came over her, the loss of her husband ate at her marrow. The terrible thing she knew about herself, but never thought of, never said in words to herself or anyone, hung at the edge of her thoughts, coming closer than it had ever dared before.

She picked up everything she saw on her desk and carried it, three trips in all to complete the act, into the kitchen. She opened the back door and threw it all into the cans that waited in the hallway. She threw her coffee cup into the sink, breaking the porcelain and startling the housekeeper who knew better than to say anything at all.

Now her desktop was clear. There was a framed photo of her husband on one corner that faced her. There was a laptop computer opened before her although she only checked her email communications from her institute or the publisher of her two books who was waiting and would wait for her third. Her appointment book was placed on one side. There was the large vase with dried flowers in it on the far end of the desk and other than that the space was clear, geometric. The golden wood on the desk was polished to a smooth honey color, glistening in the sunlight from the park. Dr. Berman felt settled, clearer. She would focus on her patient, whoever it was, who would ring the bell momentarily.

And in the early afternoon it was Edith. Edith with a pale rose lipstick and her size twelve oxford shoes. It was Edith with her hair washed and makeup covering the acne that had made a permanent home on her chin. It was Edith with hope in her heart. Dr. Berman would have read her poems over the weekend, a weekend which had seemed longer than usual to Edith, a weekend in which no matter how often she looked at her kitchen clock, the hours were moving at a geologic pace, eon after eon, layer upon layer, until Edith thought she might be a fossil, frozen in limestone.

As she approached Dr. Berman's apartment house, she had been grabbed by a familiar need, a desperate famine came upon her, not exactly a call for food by an empty stomach, not exactly a cry for nourishment by the cells and veins and muscles of her body, but more as if a creature within were howling in desperation, in need of rescue, as if it had been pinned down on the bottom of a well and the rainwater was beginning to pour in. It was a trapped feeling, as if there were no way out of the well. Her need was so great she could only pacify it with calorie after calorie, icing and bread, candy and potatoes. Edith had not been able to describe this panic to Dr. Berman yet, because she was ashamed. But it was in the poems and now Dr. Berman would know, would understand.

But when Edith sat down in the chair she saw immediately that her poems were not on the desk. She waited for Dr. Berman to mention them. She told Dr. Berman it had been a long weekend and she told her that her mother had asked her to go to a movie with her, a French film, but she had decided to stay home. She did not like going to the movies. She could feel the judging eyes of others on her as she walked to her seat and attempted to fit herself into its confines. She waited. Dr. Berman said nothing.

Of course, thought Edith, she wants me to ask her. And so she did. Did you read my poems? asked Edith. Dr. Berman was puzzled. She was silent. Edith said, I was wondering what you thought of my poems.

Dr. Berman wondered if Edith had a poem published in the paper or in a weekly magazine. She said nothing.

Edith said, You said you would read my poems. Edith thought this must be a test of her ability to assert herself, to own her work.

Dr. Berman said, I will read them when you give them to me.

Edith was silent. She looked all around the office for her three notebooks. They were not on the table behind the couch. They were not on the windowsill.

I gave you my poems, she said in her smallest voice.

I have no poems of yours, said Dr. Berman, quite certain.

nine

Gerald had a girlfriend.

The two of them smoked in the park after school. You know what they smoked. Often.

But who were they? What would they do when the action started? Could this boy take the heat and emerge a warrior? His grades were mediocre. He needed tutoring in math. He liked baseball. He played poker but without swagger. He was the kid at the table who would fold if you just smiled to yourself as if you were pretending to hide your smile, when you were in fact flashing it right at him. He wished he had been born black. He spoke sometimes in street kid slang, clearly a bluff. He was not black. He was not down with a gang. He went away to a college in Vermont where the admissions director said he wasn't interested in SATs but was looking for applicants with a love of nature and a commitment to a better world. Gerald was not so fond of nature, he did hope for a better world but after the Christmas vacation of his freshman year he dropped out.

How far a drop is that? Time would tell.

His mother, Dr. Estelle Berman, was upset, deeply upset. She wanted him to rise in a world she knew was hard on sweet souls, and would chew him up if he didn't have the necessary armor. He was not a dog to send into a dogfight. She sent him into therapy with a trusted colleague. Perhaps his aggression was inhibited. Perhaps he could find a path of his own with some help. His father thought he might like to travel awhile. Gerald was happy to lie in bed in his childhood room and watch late night TV. He was especially fond of horror movies, although he also appreciated alien figures with many heads and multiple tongues.

Dr. Berman thought his interest in these movies was his way of repressing hostility toward her.

What Gerald wanted for his life? He had no idea.

What his mother wanted for his life: She wanted to take him away to a far-off island where he could go surfing every day. He loved surfing.

His girlfriend had a rich father. This Dr. Berman considered in Adrienne's favor. There are worse ways to become rich than marrying money. Society is always shifting people up a floor or down ten through marriage. Dr. Berman understood that marriages don't always last but that they most often left the poorer partner richer. She approved of this romance that had begun in high school but lasted past the prom.

Dr. Berman was wealthy enough by herself to support their only son in a comfortable manner for the rest of his life. But Dr. Berman worried about reverses. Stock markets tumble downwards. Businesses are only as solid as last year's net. Airplanes that have flown a thousand times across the Atlantic sea burst into flames with total disregard for their passengers and their ids, egos, and superegos: defense systems, projections, phobias, libidos, memories, fame and fortune, ignominy, murderous thoughts all gone in a flash.

Gerald lifted weights and enjoyed a long night of substance use, if not abuse. He deserved a good and easy life. The children of Dr. Barman's friends and colleagues who were at Yale or Harvard Law School were pressed to join hedge funds and consulting firms but Gerald who was a dreamer needed a well-funded uncomplaining, unambitious, but attractive partner to cushion his moods, to fulfill his desires: maybe Adrienne.

Gerald was twenty-three and Adrienne was twenty-four when they were married. The wedding took place in a great room with windows overlooking the city from all 360 degrees. With a champagne glass in one hand and a canapé of egg and sturgeon you could circle about. You could see the Hudson River darkly sliding toward the sea and you could watch the East River, sluggishly moving barge after barge, through the channels that separated the auto repair shops of Long Island City from the high-rises that clung to the promenades on the Manhattan side and you could see the Pepsi-Cola sign and the Citicorp building at the gateway to the expressway that led to the Hamptons where Ralph Lauren had a store on main street and Tiffany's sold Gerald the engagement ring he had given to Adrienne.

Gerald stamped on the glass wrapped in a napkin with all his might. It would be mortifying if the crack of the glass did not resound loudly for all to hear. The rabbi explained that this broken glass was splintered by the force of the groom's foot to remind the guests that Jerusalem was lost to the Romans and its people were in exile. The psychoanalysts in the room, Gerald's mother for example, thought that the broken glass was a reminder of the seal of purity that a young girl kept sacred for her wedding night. That was the old way.

The new way happened when Adrienne was on a teen tour of Provence after her sophomore year.

The musicians stamped and screamed and the beat was louder than the trumpets that brought down Jericho and it was impossible to hear or speak over the drums. At the psychoanalysts' table the guests sat in pain, Bach lovers, operagoers, fans of Ella Fitzgerald, they stared down at their plates, like children in detention. Throughout the meal one of them, an amateur flute player, had put his hands over his ears despite his wife's reproachful look. Others sat politely until the salad course and then, like a flock of startled geese, rose and left, before the toasts.

Gerald's marriage allowed him to avoid the nagging question of self, worthy or not, guilty or not. Ready or not, here comes the world. Adrienne let her blonde straight hair grow as long as it would. Gerald sometimes felt he could climb to safety on her hair, he could pull himself up to a tower and rescue her from a witch who had imprisoned her there. His daydreams and his wet dreams were fused with the smell of her Body Shop shampoo, which came from a famine-prone African country. It was made of flowers found in the deepest bush.

On weekends they liked to walk along Madison Avenue and stare in the windows at dresses and leather bags, shoes with spike heels, furs and chinaware. Adrienne knew the names and prices of all the items they surveyed. Fendi, Wang, Manolo Blahnik, Searle. If Madison Avenue stores were each a nation with a flag she would have many stamps on her passport. Adrienne stopped to buy a pair of purple leather gloves in a little shop and Gerald wandered into a gallery nearby. He saw a metal welded shape. He stared at it. He liked it. He wanted it. It was too much money.

As he was walking out of the gallery into his mind came another shape. I could make that, he thought, but he didn't know how, which is why he enrolled in the Art Students League and discovered that he liked large canvases and small brushes that would let his hand follow his mind's eye. His mother was pleased. Adrienne was pleased. She liked hanging out in the places they now hung out. Gerald didn't expect great success. He was content to be in his class with the others, to weld in the afternoon and to paint in the morning. Therefore many of his classmates admired him. He woke up eager and he went to bed tired and his dreams went unremembered and were probably uneventful. He could be silent for hours and no one cared, no one said, What are you thinking?

Gerald walked through the East Village and held Adrienne's hand and he was happy.

Adrienne's mother moved to Barcelona with her decorator. Her father took a mistress close to Adrienne's age and Dr. Berman spoke of male jealousy of the suckling infant and in addition considered that actual incest might have been inflicted on Adrienne. It is true that this happens far more often than most people want to believe, but in this case the father would never, had never, and his generosity to his daughter, his willingness to house her in the most fashionable neighborhood in town, was not an expression of guilt as Dr. Berman suspected but merely an extension of the gargantuan largesse he had always expressed toward his own.

Gerald liked going home to Adrienne and tumbling her into their bed and turning the music up as high as it would go and doing things that people do when time seems to be on their side and fortune, good fortune, theirs for the taking. Adrienne had a drawer full of intimate apparel. If Gerald had believed in giving thanks, he would have given thanks for that drawer, or perhaps to that drawer.

Adrienne would often meet a friend for a long lunch. Pedicures and hair colorings, catalogs and daydreams filled her long days. She didn't cook although the wedding presents had included all she might need to open a five-star restaurant. At night they ordered in from the local Indian restaurant or they went out downtown.

Then Adrienne wanted a baby. Her friends were having babies. It was time. Dr. Berman referred Adrienne to the best OBGYN doctor at her hospital. It started right then. Dr. Estelle Berman kept forgetting the name of the OBYGN. She thought the name was repressed because she was jealous that her own time for procreation was long gone. She thought it was a sign of how difficult it was to accept the aging body and the narrowing of the road. But rapidly it became more than that and the list of forgotten places, dates, names, directions, affiliations, faces became longer and longer. In the privacy of her bedroom, she knew what was happening, but as soon as she knew she ignored what she knew. It must not, it could not, and it should not be. In her kitchen in the Hamptons, the housekeeper tipped over the sugar bowl on the counter and Dr. Berman entered to see a swarm of ants in the sugar, black spots on pure white, and she knew what was happening in her brain, but she would tell no one.

The child was growing in Adrienne's womb and Adrienne spent long hours naked in front of the mirror.

Gerald said, My mother is losing her mind. Adrienne said, She has too much mind, she can afford to lose a little. Gerald liked the smell of his pregnant wife. He liked the way her nipples rose to greet him. He was getting better at perspective, line, and shadow. He wasn't so shy anymore. He talked about the Giants and the Yanks and during March he talked about March madness and he talked to the women in his class about Adrienne and the drawer in which she kept the baby clothes she had received in a shower.

A boy was born in the early morning hours. Adrienne slept as her shocked body prepared itself to deliver milk to the infant who lay under a heating lamp in the nursery. The infant's thoughts, like a watercolor painting, wordless but constant, were not sharply separated from the dreams that came and went amid the air that went in and out of his small but perfect lungs. Dr. Berman was pleased the child was male. Life would be easier for him. His name was Ryan, an Irish name Adrienne had picked from a baby-naming book.

Gerald held the baby in his arms for a photograph and felt strong and sure of himself as he had never before.

Adrienne had sufficient funds. Gerald needed space and so he went to his studio and sometimes stayed there late into the night. The nursemaid took the baby to the park. Adrienne had lunch downtown with her friends. It was in a restaurant on Spring Street that she met the director of a theater group in need of backing in order to continue producing the cutting-edge, the most important, truly relevant work. The words he used were not familiar to Adrienne, but they were hypnotic along with his intense eyes and shaved head.

The sex was also sweaty and almost violent, pure and followed by monologues, Lear, King Richard, Hamlet, recited from memory. This was how Adrienne came to know that Gerald knew nothing about the theater and would never be anyone important.

By the time Adrienne moved out with three-year-old Ryan and his nanny and Gerald was forced to move into his studio, Dr. Berman was not reading her psychoanalytic journals. Nothing new, she said, as she tossed them into a pile behind her desk, but she could no longer follow, sentence by sentence, paragraph into paragraph, as if the algae in a pond had grown so thick that the bottom was obscured and the noxious gas was rising to the surface.

And then there were fewer patients. Then there were no more referrals. Then there were no more patients. She had explained to each of the remaining ones, she wasn't well, would send them to someone else, someone trusted, esteemed by her institute, someone respected by the great names that had gone before. She would not abandon her patients but finally they had gone.

And then the housekeeper left and was replaced by a woman from an agency whose name may have been Dora or maybe not. And then another woman came in the afternoon who wanted her to go out for a walk in the park although she did not want to go out at all. She had her reasons. Her son called. Yes, yes, she said to her son, I'm going to dinner tonight at Marybeth's. She wasn't going to dinner but perhaps she was or would have liked to, or might consider it one day. She had always believed in deception. It was a survival skill. Honesty was for children who didn't believe in it either.

Dr. Berman even forgot that the day Ryan was born gray fog had drifted up the two rivers that held the city in their arms.

Gerald went home, but not right away. He took a small studio in an abandoned bakery in Long Island City. The ceilings were tin and the moldings were delicate vines and the river was only a few blocks away. Lying in his bed he could see legs, women's legs, men's legs, large and small dogs, passing by. He put up shades and an iron grate on the windows. Gerald felt safe there. He also could afford the rent. He had a small income from his father and his mother was always able to give him whatever he needed. He needed just a little.

Most Saturday nights Adrienne called Gerald and asked him to take Ryan and keep him until Sunday afternoon. Gerald bought a little bed. He spent hours looking at his son, holding him. He played "Lucy in the Sky with Diamonds" again and again for the boy. Other than Ryan he was alone. Once or twice a month he went to the Central Park West apartment to see his mother. She seemed pleased to see him but often conversation stalled and he went into the den and watched a ball game.

The doormen still knew him. The caretaker from the visiting nurse service and the maid greeted him with smiles. But at the center of the apartment, in her large living room, on her red velvet couch, his mother sat, nodding at him, restless, a leg bouncing up and down impatiently, not wanting to say the wrong thing but unsure of the purpose of the visit. Still he came.

His mother was a vanishing mother. Blessed by a hopeful nature, he bet on the scores of football games, basketball games. Hope was his wild card. He held it close to his chest.

Of course, hope is a fine friend but not a sufficient one. Gerald needed the stars to smile on him and stars are most indifferent to wishes no matter how many children send their twinkling voices upwards toward the heavens. A painting of his, a nude classmate sitting on the edge of a bed, was selected for a show in a small gallery in St. Albans but it was not noticed by the one critic who did make it to the opening.

Fear took hope's place. He started to refer to himself as a starving artist. He was not starving but he was badly in need of attention. Gerald took stock. Enough was enough. He needed to be careful for Ryan's sake. Not that Ryan needed his father for economic safety but Ryan needed a father he could respect, a man of the world, like Gerald's father, who had had a chauffeur drive him to work each day. Above all else Gerald did not want to disappoint Ryan.

His mother smiled at him when he took out his phone and showed her photos of his child. Her smile was vague. Gerald had wanted more, more enthusiasm, more affection. But his mother had never been the sentimental kind. She allowed Lily to sit on her pillow, to knead her blanket, to sleep under the sheets, but she was not overly fond of any activity that might cause stains on a dress or a carpet. When he brought Ryan himself to visit her on a Sunday afternoon, she seemed to wake up, staring at the child. She asked for tea and cookies and she offered them to Ryan. What should she say to the child? What games could she remember? She wanted to give the child something special. She asked for her jewelry box and she opened it and gave Ryan a necklace to have for his own. When he tried to put it back in the box, she stopped him, No, no, that's for you.

Later, Gerald took it from the child who protested with loud tears, and returned it to its rightful place.

Gerald took over his mother's finances. He paid the bills online. He paid the help each week and he made sure that all accounts were current. He spoke with the lawyer his father had used and he spoke with the tax accountant. Perhaps, said the lawyer, your mother would be more comfortable in a home, an assisted-living facility, where she might benefit from the stimulation of others. Also, said the lawyer, the medical care might be better. In case, you know, the lawyer waved his hand, unwilling or unable to name the calamities that might lie ahead.

Gerald considered the lawyer's advice. It would be easier if his mother's care was not subject to the vagaries of a visiting nurse, or a second maid, or the kindness of the cook who had been with the family long before Dr. Berman began to have trouble naming the foods she wanted for dinner. But there was the problem of the apartment itself, the wonderful rent-controlled apartment. It was Gerald's childhood home. If his mother vacated the apartment it would go on the market at current rental prices. Gerald decided to move back into his own bedroom. If he stayed in the apartment for a sufficient number of years while his mother still lived there he could stay forever at the low price, less than he was paying for his studio. The lawyer meant well enough but his mother would have to stay and he would move in with her. One of the rooms he could make his studio. One day management might pay him a significant sum to leave the rent-controlled apartment and he could live somewhere far away. He understood the value of the large rooms, the pantry, the cabinets that had been built in, the view of the park, the subway down the block, the high ceilings, the uniformed doormen.

Gerald was now fond of country music. All through the rooms the sound of Patsy Cline and Johnny Cash thundered. In the hallway, in front of the now unused office, a long metal shape reached almost to the ceiling. It was a tree he had created from parts of an abandoned automobile. It seemed to have crystal tears emerging from its red trunk that had once been a fender of a Camry. Dr. Berman kept telling the aide to remove the tree. The aide agreed again and again but the tree was there, Gerald's tree of life. Take it away, Dr. Berman said, she spoke her desire in a whisper and then in a scream. But Gerald paid no attention to the request, no matter how many times it was repeated.

He played his music as loudly as possible to soothe the thing in him that ached all night long and went stomping around after midnight. There were sparks of hope. A gallery owner had complimented him. There was a group show that had not yet eliminated him. There was always hope, bruised, bent, but rising up again and again.

Sometimes when Gerald came home in the afternoon and opened the door he smelled the stale air of the apartment and also the faint but clear scent of urine, also ammonia used to eradicate that very smell. Sometimes Gerald smelled even less pleasant odors. His mother had begun to resist the changing of underthings.

She used her nails to attack. She used her voice to demand and order the caretakers to leave her alone. She threatened to fire them. There was no use in trying. If clean things were left by her side so she could put them on herself, she simply put them on over whatever was soiled underneath. The odors made their way through the layers of clothing. The night aide left her alone. The morning aide tried to coax or divert her attention with chatter and sometimes she succeeded but often she did not. Some days skirts and blouses were pulled on over nightgowns and on top of several of the awkward and dreadful napkins she wore all at once. Some mornings she was washed and some mornings she refused. It had come to that.

Gerald discovered that unpleasant smells were worse when first encountered but then within a half hour the mind or senses grew accustomed to them and he was easily able to ignore the odors that followed his mother in her restless wanderings from room to room.

He lay in his childhood bed listening to Tammy Wynette yearning as he once yearned but perhaps not for the same thing.

Gerald took an extra long time in the shower each morning. All his clothes went to the cleaners after one wearing. He used a strong aftershave. He worried that some odor would cling to him, embarrass him.

What he wanted to do was become a recognized artist. He wanted his work to be worthy of respect and envy and dollars, many dollars, so many that they would support him and Ryan forever after, perhaps on a Caribbean island with palm trees, white sand, and a turquoise sea, casting white spray on a nearby jetty. Tourists would come to see his work and they would want to purchase it and he would let them, sometimes, if he liked them.

In the meantime he breathed in the air filled with the smells of incontinence. He kissed his mother good morning and he brought her a glass of milk in her bedroom as she settled in for the night.

If the owners of the building should decide to convert their property into a tenant-owned entity—well then, the pot of gold at the end of that rainbow would become his and his alone.

Yes, Ryan was a child of divorce and Dr. Berman, at other moments during her long practice of psychiatry, would have made certain dire predictions based on that fact, but he was a sweet cheerful boy with trusting eyes and a love of Thomas the Tank Engine, who slept with him in his bed whether he was with his mother or his father. Two days a week he spent with his father in the rambling apartment opposite the park. On those days his father took him to the playground and to the zoo where they watched the penguins diving in a tank. Gerald held the child's hand and promised him that one day he would buy him an airplane of his very own. He bought Ryan a drum set and seemed not to mind the loud noises that went on and on as Ryan thumped and jumped about.

The nights Ryan slept over in the small bed that Gerald had installed in the fourth bedroom, Gerald stayed home. He watched videos with Ryan until the child fell asleep in his lap on the couch. Often he lay down with Ryan and stroked his hair and patted his arm as the hours of the night went by. In her bedroom his mother lay under her covers, dreaming. Could she recognize herself in her dreams or were they too fading, turning gray, pale, and indistinct? Or were her dreams nightmares in which the falling of things crushed her bones again and again? In the morning she forgot her dreams.

The caretaker slept on a wide plush chair in Dr. Berman's bedroom. Gerald had taken the large oak dining table and sent it along with the chairs to an auction house. He sold the cabinet that held the silverware and the sconces that had decorated the walls. In the room he put a climbing gym for Ryan and a toy box and a tricycle and he decorated the room with posters of the Giants and the Jets. In the room he used as a studio the carpet was gone, the walls were covered with sketches and blank paper and spots where Gerald had splashed paint or dripped down or simply swiped at space as he thought his wordless thoughts.

When Ryan looked up at his father he saw the muscles he might have one day. When he was at his father's house he played with his football, tossing it under the furniture and fetching it back again and again.

The housekeeper had her own room but she was not always

there anymore. It was hard to tell if she was doing her work or was just pretending.

Dr. Berman's friend Louise still came to visit from time to time. Louise believed that her friend was pleased to see her. Sometimes she would say Louise's name. Once Dr. Berman asked after Louise's daughter. Louise brought chocolates and sometimes flowers. The apartment where for over a quarter of a century psychoanalysts had gathered after meetings, come to dinner when arriving from Rome or Paris or Switzerland, was now filled with echoes as if in another dimension, an invisible party went on and on, someone ridiculing someone else's attempt at an explanation of the mirroring of some cathexis or other. Someone was complaining that someone else was overrated and someone was trying very hard to please the elders of the congregation, to impress and to shine. Now the walls were dingy and the carpet worn. Gerald was avoiding the expense of repair. Once every two weeks the hairdresser came. Gerald could not bear to see the dull gray roots emerging from his mother's scalp. He saw death coming with each quarter of an inch of stiff hair.

Louise also suggested to Gerald that his mother might do better in a home where her condition was understood. Perhaps some companionship would improve her spirit. Gerald wanted his mother to stay just where she was.

She wants to stay here, he said.

Real estate, said Louise.

Yes, thought Gerald.

When Gerald thought of Ryan, he knew he had to be clear about his goals, sharp of mind, free of drugs, and only on the nights when Ryan was with his mother would he drink and then in front of the television, watching late night shows, he would float like a jettisoned boat cushion on the waves of a dark ocean, all through the long night, no shore visible, sky without stars.

A woman in his class invited him to show two of his paintings with her and four friends. They were going to have an open house at one of their studios in downtown Brooklyn.

Would he join them for dinner on Saturday night just to see if the chemistry would work? Yes, said Gerald. His mother's aide would babysit for Ryan for a few extra dollars.

Gerald wore his non-paint-splattered jeans. He put on a dark blue sweater that Adrienne had once said made him look like a movie star. He shaved carefully. His blue eyes, his mother's blue eyes, were clear. He was ready. His mother was sitting at her small table in the room that had once been her office. She had insisted that this table be set with her best silverware each evening and the candles lit promptly at seven o'clock as they had been whenever she was home, not going to meetings, not teaching a class, not going to the theater or a benefit or a book party. The white tablecloth now had some rips in the corner. The aide covered these with a napkin.

Outside, the darkness fell over the park and the lamplights shined on the occasional dog walker wrapped in scarves and down coats. Behind them the Time Warner building shone its white light and the Empire State sent its blue needle up to the moon.

Ryan was in his bed. His father had told him he would be back later. But suddenly later seemed too late. His grandmother's nurse had gone into the kitchen and was eating her own dinner. His father had not read him a bedtime story. He had forgotten and Ryan had not asked for it. His father was in a rush to get somewhere. But now, in his dinosaur shirt, his blue pajama bottoms, he was unable to sleep. He felt strange, was he hungry? He thought that perhaps that was it.

He opened the door to his room. He thought he might phone his mother. He wanted to hear her voice. Go to sleep, little moose, she would say. He knew the number of her cell phone by heart, but he wasn't supposed to call for no reason. Did he have a good reason? He thought not. The hall was dark. A light reflected from an open kitchen door let Ryan see the path to the main entrance and from there he could see that his grandmother was sitting at a table, a glass of wine in front of her.

Dr. Berman, he announced, I'm here, as he walked toward the table. He didn't want to call her Mom, as his father did. Everyone else in the household called her Dr. Berman, so he thought he should too.

Dr. Berman was startled out of her reverie. Her father had kept a bottle of brandy in his office, which he kept hidden under a pile of newspapers. She preferred sherry, Bristol Cream. In her thoughts there was the sound of thunder and rain on the windowpanes. There were owls in the house. Had there ever been owls in the house? Of course not, but Dr. Berman kept seeing owls. One was sitting on her father's knee, its cold yellow eyes staring at her. She pressed her hands against her face. She knew certainly there had never been owls in the house. Dr. Berman, said Ryan again, and he tugged at her sleeve so she would see him. She looked down. She saw him. Who are you? she said. She used her official voice, a reprimand, a dismissal, a threat, a voice of authority drawing a line, a line that must not be crossed.

You know, the child answered.

Tell me again, she said.

Ryan, he said.

She looked him over carefully. Who sent you? she said.

No one, he answered.

Why are you here? she asked, her voice steady, even.

Ryan considered. After a long pause he said, It's Saturday.

The candlelight reflected in the window, the orange flame reproduced in a line leading out over the park, a flickering line.

The aide in the kitchen finished her steak and string beans and sweet potato and scraped her plate and was rinsing it in the sink.

Gerald was talking about a good place to buy sound equipment for a stereo system. There was gossip about another student who had been taken to the hospital the week before. He could feel his legs trembling under the table, but his face was calm and he was careful to drink slowly, to stay alert. He wanted to be liked. He wanted to be included in their plans.

Ryan looked up at the table. He stood on his toes. He saw a roll, a dinner roll on a china plate. I'm hungry, he said. And Dr. Berman saw that he wanted her roll. She saw him staring at it. She didn't see a child. She saw the jaws and the teeth of the enemies she had always known would one day come to tear apart her flesh, rip open her chest, take her heart. It wasn't a shape anymore. It was a tornado coming closer, ready to take from her what was hers, her life, her self, her hopes. It wasn't her id, it wasn't her superego or her ego or her narcissistic object relations or her masochistic failures or sadistic fantasies. It wasn't obsession, repression, negative or positive transference. It was them, the them that had always been out there waiting, and now they had come: crawled out of the abyss, ready to destroy her. There they were. They were owls with sharp little beaks.

She pushed back her chair and took the burning candle out of its silver holder. She took a second to watch the flame. It was a strong flame, steady as her breath. She saw her red chipped nails against the candle's long stem.

She reached down and on the shirtsleeve, where a Tyrannosaurus rex was cut in half by the repeating pattern, she set the candle to the fabric and then before the child could run or cry she lit the front of his shirt and his hair. The child looked at his grandmother and pressed himself against her skirt. The child screamed. He looked like a burning bush: a bush without the voice of God. His grandmother waved the candle in the air. The aide in the kitchen was talking to her cousin in Jamaica on her cell phone. There were small fires springing up the seams of the curtains by the time she came into the room. Black smoke drove her back. The firemen came up the back stairs. They were too late.

Lily was found seared but alive under a bed. She did not last through the night.

The aide was afraid she would be blamed. No one blamed her.

Six months later the apartment, ransomed by the building's owner for a significant sum, was listed in the Sunday *New York Times* at full market price and was sold to an airline executive and his young third wife and her two daughters from a previous marriage who took the bus across town to go to school at the Convent of the Sacred Heart, the school that Jacqueline Bouvier Kennedy Onassis herself had attended once upon a time.

Dr. Z. said, The institute should establish a memorial lecture in her name.

Dr. H. said, I don't think so.

Dr. Z. said, We should do something in her honor.

Dr. H. said, Let's make sure every classroom is equipped with a fire extinguisher.

ten

The very young analyst found himself thinking about his colleague, Dr. Leah Brewster. She was in his class at the institute. She did not wear a wedding ring. She was in her thirties and had gone to medical school in the Midwest near her home in Ohio. Some magnetic impulse had brought her to New York, to psychoanalysis, to his class. She was taller than he was. She was forever biting at her thumb when she was concentrating. She had eyes that seemed to both hide and reveal her at once. She was sexual like a cat, a little plump, and her full breasts appeared, demurely appeared, at the open edges of her blouses. She wore a locket around her neck like a little girl, but she clearly wasn't a little girl. And the very young analyst, who certainly loved his wife and children, couldn't help it, week after week, sitting next to her around a table, discussing with total dispassion the questions of inversions and perversions, the role of the masochistic fantasy. He had fallen in love.

He told his analyst. He hadn't approached her. He hadn't let her know, but he felt that she knew. How was it possible that his thermostat could be up so high and she not feel his longing? And where had his desire for his wife gone? He was always too tired, it was too late, one of the children was still awake. He was distracted. His lovely wife, his good wife, bored him. Oh God, she bored him.

And so the tale took on a familiar literary plot. John Cheever had written it over and over again. Tolstoy, Updike, Bellow. There was a time when every week *The New Yorker* published another story about infidelity, desire wandering through the cocktail party, and the subtle, hinted-at, common human unhappiness that made its home in the marriage bed. It was so trite, his love, or was it lust, for Dr. Leah Brewster. He suddenly hated the sameness, the sameness of everything. No, not everything, just his wife, the way she ate a health bar for breakfast every morning. The way she still wore her college sweatshirt to bed on cold nights. The way she wanted to visit her parents whenever they had a few days they might go someplace interesting. The way she smelled of formaldehyde from her lab sometimes: not often he had to admit. Sometimes when they went out to dinner with friends she wore too much makeup. He could see it caked underneath her eyes.

If his wife were killed crossing the street, a truck delivering electronics veering fast around the corner, catching her as she stepped from the curb, then he would reach out to his colleague and what would be more natural, two analysts, working side by side. They could take an office together with a shared waiting room, their winter jackets pressing against each other in the coat closet. It's just a fantasy, he said to his analyst, who said, There is no "just" when it comes to fantasies.

His wife was a research scientist at Sloan Kettering. Her admired her skill, her mind. He came home early to put the children to bed when she went off to give a paper at this conference or that. She was always cleaning surfaces. She saw bacteria where he saw crumbs but he had become used to her habits. Now he complained about them. She is too neat, he complained to his analyst. It borders on obsessive behavior, he added. She hates dogs, he said. I think it would be good for the children to have a dog.

Do you think Leah would keep the dishes in the sink for days on end and you would be happier? asked his analyst.

He sighed. Sometimes it was so hard to make Dr. H. understand. Was the man dense, the wrong analyst for him, incapable of human empathy? He told his analyst these thoughts.

Uh-huh, said the analyst.

And the winter went on. The oldest child was learning to read. The youngest child was almost out of diapers. The holidays came and were spent with his wife's parents in Massachusetts. His own patients suffered because of the happiness of others and complained about their New Year's parties or lack of them, their parents, their friends, their own aches that he had not been able to banish.

At last the evergreen wreaths on the doors of buildings turned brown. The streets were littered with trees with aluminum icicles blowing in the breezes and dead needles falling to the gutter, waiting for the sanitation trucks to pick up the debris of celebrations that the young analyst, like a robot, moved through untouched.

She's brilliant, Dr. Leah Brewster, he said to his analyst.

That explains it, came the answer from the chair behind his head.

Last night, he said, as we were getting undressed, the mother of my children started to talk about a colleague of hers who was trying to get pregnant, had lost a few early pregnancies, was going to try fertility treatments, and she gave me all the stats and the odds and the dangers of adoption. I stopped listening. Do I care about her colleague's womb? I hear enough during the day. I don't need this just as we are getting into bed. I know, he said to his analyst, I sound like a beast. His analyst was silent.

He was too young for a midlife crisis. He was however not too young or too old for the old wounds of his childhood to appear again. His analyst expected that the storm would soon arrive in full force.

Maybe I should ask her to go for coffee with me, he said to his analyst, and waited for some reaction.

And then, said his analyst, what happens then?

And he didn't go near her after that week's class, but planned to very soon. He went over the scene in his head a million times. *Leah, would you like to have coffee with me before we head home?* He would say it casually. She would tell him about swimming in the lake as a child and being bitten by a giant turtle (did turtles bite? he wasn't sure). She would tell him about the man who broke her heart, a fellow medical school student who broke up with her the summer after they went to Europe together and stayed in hostels and got drunk and had sex on the sap-covered pine needles on the forest floor in Germany.

And then he and she would end up in a hotel on Lexington Avenue. He had picked it out on Google. And he would explain that he wasn't a monster. She would understand . . . Perhaps she felt the same pull toward him? Perhaps she didn't. Would he tell his wife? Sooner or later he would tell her. It would be unbearable, this secret, the fact of the other woman. She would sense it. She would know. She was already breaking out in hives for no reason at all. She said it was pressure at work, but it wasn't. It was his betrayal, which so far was just an imaginary betrayal but it hurt him, it hurt him for her, because he did not want to hurt her, although his analyst was not so sure about that. He woke often at three in the morning and lay in bed, wanting, but not wanting the woman beside him, wanting sleep.

In the sixties everyone believed in sexual freedom. Loyalty, sacrifice was very out of fashion. He was born in the early eighties when the time for orgies was over, and he believed in loyalty and sacrifice and making his children strong and happy, although he understood perfectly well that might well be impossible, human nature being so prone to calamity.

Divorce marked children, some never recovered. He didn't want to harm his children. On the other hand staying in a marriage where the spark had died, where the joy was no longer there, when you felt your home was a trap instead of a refuge, that too would harm the children.

I see you are concerned about your children, said Dr. H. Was his tone ironic?

Was it a dream he had brought to a session or had the analyst introduced the subject in some way that he hadn't noticed? But they were talking about his own father who had left the family before the young analyst was ten and had gone to another part of the country and sometimes sent birthday cards and sometimes didn't. I wonder, said Dr. H., what your father's absence has to do with your love for your wife now?

Was he reproducing in his children the pain he had felt? Was he mastering the loss by creating it himself? Was he making a mess of his marriage to send a message to his own childhood? I am master now.

What was going on?

The young analyst talked and talked and said some things he had never said before. The more he talked the less he felt compelled toward Dr. Leah Brewster, who for the long months of his passion had been unaware of her role in his fantasy life and was herself, after some hesitation, starting a relationship with a suitable man, already divorced, whom she had met on Match.com.

One April evening the young analyst came home from his office and played a game of Clue with his oldest child and read the younger one a story, turned out the light in the children's room. His wife and he sat down to dinner, a Thai dinner they had ordered.

Are you all right? she said to him because he was looking at her peculiarly.

I'm fine, he said.

Are you tired? she asked him.

No, not tired, he said, and he stood up and took her hand and led her into the bedroom, leaving the pad thai and the beef satay in their carton boxes.

Dance with me, he said.

And she did.

Later she said, I think Ronit is pregnant.

Who? he said.

You know, she said, the fertility treatment one.

That's good, he said, and closed his eyes and went to sleep.

eleven

After a year at New York University, a transfer student, majoring in classical studies, which primarily meant learning Greek and Latin and reading Ovid and Virgil and Homer, Anna Fishbein had become convinced that humanity was not always pitiful and that language was often a comfort. She now saw herself as part of a long story, still unfolding. However she still had bad days when she lost her way and a deep loneliness drove her to hide in her dorm room. This loneliness seemed unshakable. She could no longer see Dr. Berman. Something had happened to Dr. Berman. She had felt deserted, betrayed, and had spent a week or so feeling unlucky, permanently unlucky, but then her mother had arranged for her to see Dr. Z.

She liked him. He listened to her and his voice echoed in her head as she dressed in the morning, as she rode the subway to class, as she sat in the library and paused in her note-taking. She really liked him. She knew it was transference. She knew her relationship with him was pretend, pretend for a purpose, the purpose to heal her. She was willing to be healed. It was hard, sometimes it was very hard. She did not like the things she was learning about herself. Sometimes she liked them so little she forgot them entirely, erased her memory of the last session, so everything had to be said again and again.

And so it was when she met Mary Rose O'Brian who was pre-med and friends with a faculty member in the Classics Department who invited everyone to an annual Christmas party at her home. Mary Rose was tall and broad. She had large feet like Cinderella's evil stepsister. She was not shy like Anna. She had a loud voice and a very deep laugh. She had wide shoulders and when she walked she stepped firmly, she moved like an ice cutter through the Antarctic. There was no one who was going to mess with Mary Rose. She wore an army jacket and sometimes she wore a blue striped tie. She was what she was and a lock of her hair kept falling into her eyes and she kept brushing it away and when she looked at Anna a strange new electric pulse ran through Anna's body. It was not an unpleasant feeling.

Which is how the two women found themselves eating Mexican food in a small restaurant near Anna's dorm. It was how they talked to each other about their families, about their favorite movies, about the admiration Mary Rose felt for the beauty of nature. They talked about swimming in cold lakes and both of them disliked Florida where Mary Rose's parents had moved and Anna had received a nasty sunburn one vacation when she was nine.

At the end of the evening when they parted outside of Anna's dorm they did not touch but the possibility hung in the air. It made Anna anxious but not unhappy.

It took Anna several weeks before she told Dr. Z. about Mary Rose. She expected he would have some stuffy damning Freudian response, but instead he asked, What do you feel when you are with her? Anna told him. That's good, he said. That is all good. Anna could practically hear him purr.

Maybe that was just the radiator.

Have I made a bad choice? Anna asked him.

What do you think? he asked her.

She blushed.

I'm okay, she said.

Good, he said.

I'm really okay, she said.

That is really good, he said.

And so it went through the semester and the one after that. In the summer Mary Rose and Anna both had jobs as a counselors at a nearby day camp. The two shared a small apartment above a garage and Mary Rose and Anna together went to work every morning and to bed at night. They watched summer reruns on an old television and listened to music on their iPods and went swimming on the weekends at the local public beach. Under the water they held hands and when they surfaced they pulled at each other's bathing suits and tossed seaweed in each other's faces. At such times it would be hard to tell how old they were. Were they sisters? The tall one was older or maybe not.

Anna's parents spent August on the Cape. Come with your friend, they said. The family crisis had come and gone. Anna was independent, making up for lost time. Yes, there were a few white scars on her arms. Yes, her mother listened to her voice carefully, always hoping not to hear what she might hear. Meyer was at Stanford, something about zebra fish and brain tissue.

I know what my life will be like, Anna told Dr. Z. Mary Rose and I have plans. After I graduate we are going to get married. We're going to move to a village in Vermont and I'm going to open a bakery and Mary Rose will go on to study forestry, and then when she has her degree we're going to have two or maybe three children. I'm going to carry them and Mary Rose will donate the egg so the children will be both of ours. In the winter the children will ski to school, said Anna. Sounds like a fairy-tale life, said Dr. Z.

And then one night in a bar called Barney's after a famous woman who dressed in men's clothes and in the 1920s lived in Paris and was a daring beauty before such beauty could show itself all over town, Mary Rose saw a young woman wearing high black boots and a shirt that had a drawing of a racing car over the left pocket. Anna knew nothing about car racing. Mary Rose did. Anna put her hand on Mary Rose's arm. Mary Rose didn't even turn around, she shook off Anna's hand and leaned toward the racing car as if gravity were pulling her hand and there was nothing she could do to stop its forward motion.

Outside the bar the last of the smokers were puffing into the night. Anna waited for Mary Rose but she didn't appear. Anna went back to their apartment. She left the car for Mary Rose. She walked past the 7-Eleven and the gas station with its cold white lights and the Dairy Queen shuttered against the dark. Her limbs were tired. She hated Mary Rose but not as much as she loved her. She realized she was stomping around after midnight. She did not take a razor to her arm but she remembered how that felt and the memory accompanied her all through the night and the next day when Mary Rose appeared she took one look at Anna's face and said, Darling, nothing lasts forever. A little longer, said Anna. We'll always be friends, said Mary Rose. No we won't, said Anna. Mary Rose was sorry, but not sorry enough.

I'll never love anyone again, Anna said to Dr. Z. For better or worse, said Dr. Z., you will.

No, said Anna.

Yes, said Dr. Z. He had the last word because the session was over.

Do you know, said Dr. Z. to Dr. H. at the annual fund-raising party for the institute where they shared a table with their wives and a wealthy patron and his aged mother, why all the young mothers are reading that Sendak book, Where the Wild Things Are, *to their toddlers?*

Yes, said Dr. H. They want their children to know where to go if a crisis arrives.

You mean to an island? asked Dr. Z.

No, came the reply, inside of books. In the pages of books, that's where you go when trouble comes.

Dr. Z. laughed. He sloshed his wine on his pants, which was all right because it was white wine. Good drawings of the id, said Dr. Z.

An imaginary animal, said Dr. H.

Are you presenting that theory at the May meeting? asked Dr. Z.

I have no desire to be famous, said Dr. H. I'd have to chair too many committees.

twelve

Dr. Z.'s daughter was not one of those little girls who played dress-up in princess dresses, letting silver beads and purple feathers drift across the carpet. She was a chess player and very fond of puzzles. Her mother and father were careful with their children: reality was presented unadorned, no tooth fairy, no elves, and no higher power beyond Con Edison. There were piano lessons and a brief bout with Mandarin which was abandoned for shell-collecting by the beach, bird-watching and the West Side Soccer League.

Ronit was named after a grandmother who as a little girl escaped in a sixteen-foot fishing boat captained by a Dane. Dr. Z. had never been sure if this Dane who had saved his mother was a righteous man or one who demanded certain favors or funds in return. The story, like most of the stories from the other shore, was uncertain in detail, accurate in emotion, but fogged over by the mist of time and the confusions of memory.

Dr. Z. was proud of his daughter who was not overly anxious, phobic, timid, or aggressive. She was not joyless or friendless and could navigate setbacks, like not being invited to someone's birthday party, with grace. The muscles in her legs tensed as she ran and climbed and swung from high bars. She had long shiny black hair that she wore in braids until her body changed and her breasts appeared, expected but still surprising, a gift, one that came with a dark side.

And from her excellent college she went to an excellent medical school, the same one that had granted a degree to her mother some thirty years earlier. She had no interest in neurology, her mother's field, or psychiatry, her father's. She was drawn to oncology. This was where the battle against the enemy was at its fiercest, the stakes were high, the losses many. It wasn't a field for the faint of heart. Ronit wanted to go to war and she did.

Perhaps it wore on her. She seemed to reject boyfriends after a few months of promising sleepovers. One lasted a year and a half. To soft-spoken inquiries from her mother she always smiled and said she wasn't ready. Why not? asked Dr. Z., who was not only eager for a grandchild but convinced that union, sexual and otherwise, was necessary for a good life. Was this old-fashioned of him? Would he have felt the same way about his son who had in fact married before he was thirty to a woman who taught the learning-disabled and seemed in perfect harmony with her fate. Also, she baked and broiled and sautéed blissful dinners for all occasions. Not to mention birthday cakes for the children decorated with tiny plastic horses, clowns, trains riding on their chocolate tracks. Ronit ate cafeteria food in the hospital and kept a box of energy bars in her pantry for emergencies.

The family celebrated her thirty-first birthday with a picnic in the park followed by a performance of *Hamlet* under the stars. Dr. Z. wanted to ask about the men she had met, any interesting ones, any long-term possibilities. He had no ethnic or religious requirements, no specific occupations, no visions of a beloved son-in-law keeping him company in his old age.

That is not quite true, a better way to say it would be that he was ready to give up all his personal wishes for the happiness of his daughter, anyone she loved he would embrace.

Ronit had a cat she was quite fond of. Several of the young men she had dated began to sneeze and cough when settled on her couch with a glass of wine and expectations of a move into the bedroom. Ronit bid them good night, walking them politely down the long hall to the elevator. Her loyalty lay with the cat, who slept in her bed, his body giving warmth to the cold winter nights, his tongue licking her face before the alarm rang in the mornings.

A healthy life, said Freud, requires work and love. So I have half a healthy life, said Ronit to her friends when they met for drinks at the end of a very long day. Dr. Z. did not laugh when she said this to him. Perhaps you should consider therapy, he said. When, just when, asked Ronit, would I have time for that? Dr. Z. did not press her. She became chief resident, received an appointment at the hospital and published several papers on the success or lack of it of this new protocol or that. When Dr. Z. looked carefully at his daughter he saw the way her jaw tightened when she watched her nephew play with his toy doctor kit, a present from her on one family occasion. He saw that the soft shine of youth was disappearing from her skin, her hair held back by a clip was not free to bounce and flow as it once had been. He saw a few gray hairs at her crown. It was unthinkable that age should reach her, drain her, and he was helpless in the face of time, the facts of life and death could not be altered by his love. Ronit was sliding through time and she was still without a partner. Did she want a woman? Dr. Z. dared to ask. Ronit laughed at him. Oh Dad, she said, leave me alone.

Maybe if the cat would die, he thought. How old was that cat?

And then, shortly before her thirty-seventh birthday, Ronit met her father for dinner at an Italian restaurant near the hospital and before they opened the menus she said to him, I'm seeing someone. Oh, he said, using his neutral voice, his doctor voice, when a patient told him of wanting to put a knife in the heart of her sister, or of planning to hide his fortune offshore. Oh, he repeated. Ronit waited. She made him ask, Who? He asked. The man was a poet. She had met him at his mother's bedside. A poet, said Dr. Z. who admired poets in principle but considered them like rare flora, better kept at a distance, far down some Amazon river and not in one's own living room, or for that matter in one's daughter's bedroom. Is he healthy? he asked Ronit, visions of Keats and consumption passing through his mind. Nobody—not even poets—has consumption anymore, he reminded himself.

Dr. Z. said, Tell me about him. And she did, leaving out a few things, the second wife for instance, as well as the long ago stay at a rehab hospital in Minnesota. As she talked Dr. Z. saw the color rise in her face and he saw that his daughter had something else in her life besides her patients and he was relieved and would have been joyous but he had one important question to ask, before he would really allow joy to romp in his heart.

And what about children? he asked so casually he might have been asking if this prospective son-in-law liked pumpkin pie or did he prefer apple?

Yes, said Ronit, he wants children right away and so do I. And, she added, he is not allergic to cats.

There was a wedding, not too expensive, but with dancing

and Ronit's brother lifted his own child into the air and tossed him into his new brother-in-law's arms and everyone clapped and circled around. Then Dr. Z. found himself high up above the small crowd sitting on a small chair supported by six friends of the groom consisting of the entire staff of a small literary magazine. The musicians played on and on. Dr. Z. glanced over at his wife who was visibly alarmed by her suspension up in the air but nevertheless took the time to blow him a kiss, an expression of love he welcomed even in the din, even as he worried that his large and somewhat overweight body might crash to the floor, causing mayhem.

Because of that vivid thought he recognized in himself the blood red thread of regret: Ronit was no longer his alone, although it was precisely what he had hoped for, and had worried might never happen.

For the millionth time he saw in himself what he taught his patients to see in themselves, the raw other side, the dark selfish maw of his soul. Up in the air above the dancing wedding crowd he shut the door against the less pleasant part of himself which accompanied him everywhere, even to his daughter's wedding, the wedding he had waited for so long and so eagerly.

Shortly afterwards the cat developed an aneurysm in his spine and, wailing in pain, was put to sleep in an early dawn visit to the only animal hospital open in the city at 4 a.m. Ronit did not seem overly grieved. She was trying to get pregnant.

Dr. Z. did not want to ask any questions that would cross the important boundaries between a married child and her attentive father. He did not want to be the one who accompanied her to the fertility clinic when it came to that and it did come to that after twenty-one months of failure. He wanted to appease the right gods, the ones he did not believe in, so that Ronit could have a child. The poet seemed steady in his affection. He published a book that he dedicated to Ronit, giving a galley to Dr. Z. and his wife with a thank-you note for their faith in him. Faith was not Dr. Z.'s habit. But he had grown fond of the poet and when he imagined his grandchildren he thought of them like Wallace Stevens, doctor poets, poet doctors. He knew that was absurd—they might very well become football players or die in some war he himself wouldn't live to see. Nevertheless, in his daydreams as he waited for a late patient or walked home from his office, he conjured them up, reading Dante in Italian and Freud in German and giving papers at international conferences and poetry readings at the local Y.

I'm becoming a fool, he said to his wife. You always were a fool, she said, my fool.

It turned out the poet had a low sperm count. It turned out that while she was now only thirty-nine, Ronit had pushed the flexibility of her female parts to their limit. She now could hear the drip of time as month changed into month, season moved into season. Time was no longer the unnoticed river that ran through her life, it was the nightmare that woke her in the dark. The first in vitro failed. The second in vitro failed too. She had begun to stare at every pregnant woman she passed in the street. A bitter taste of envy and rue would come over her and she would look away, ashamed of herself, unable to be glad for the woman who was not her. She had trouble sleeping and in the early hours before dawn she would look over at her husband and despise him for no reason at all. The hormones she was taking in preparation for the in vitro made her emotions careen about as if they were in a perpetual car derby, smash, crash, crunch. She burst into tears when a scan of a young girl with bone cancer came back with the wrong shades. She had never done that before. She promised herself never to do that again.

And so the night before the third try she would have prayed but she had no one to pray to. Instead she called her father. He said, I have a good feeling about this. This time it will work. He didn't have a good feeling about anything but he wanted to comfort her. He wanted to spare her. You know, he said, you could adopt. I don't want to talk about that tonight, she said, and he said, I'm sorry. Good night Daddy, she said, and he felt a sharp pain in his heart. It wasn't angina. It wasn't a crucial vein closing. It was just the fact: his child in danger.

You had to wait a few days, almost a week, to see if hormone levels changed, if anything had happened in the mysterious cave of the womb. Dr. Z. rehearsed his lines. He had prepared exactly the words he would say to her if the eggs remained lifeless. He prepared his voice, he prepared his words, no man about to go into battle concentrated as fiercely on his purpose, to blunt the pain, to encourage, to simply be there, but not be intrusive. How not to be intrusive when he was, most surely, intruding. Above all he was determined not to let his daughter see or suspect his own disappointment. Also he knew that was impossible. She would know. It would add to her pain.

And so he was sitting in his chair, his doctor chair, in his office, his feet up on the stool in front of him, waiting for the bell that would announce his next patient, when the phone rang and he picked it up. What now, what now? ran through his mind as it always did. It was Ronit. He knew instantly almost before the first word was sent soaring through the air. It was the lightness of her tone, the way she said, Dad. Yes, she was pregnant. The following weeks brought her word of twins. It also brought new fears. What if they die in utero? What if they are damaged? When was the amnio? When would they know if the babies had avoided the diseases of older mothers, the dread diseases that he could recite in his mind and did each morning as he rose from his bed?

Dr. Z. had not asked the poet if his family history contained schizophrenia, manic depression, suicides, thieves, sociopaths. It would have been rude. His daughter would have been furious with him. He knew better than to ask those questions. A simple tell me about your family had produced a story of a potter mother and a father who baked bread and taught Asian history at a progressive New England college. Also he had spoken of an aunt who had died of leukemia in her thirties. Dr. Z. wasn't worried about leukemia or at least no more so than all the other threats that now gathered around his daughter. He banished them from his mind. He was too well analyzed himself, too sane to allow the normal dangers of life to spoil his pleasure, to darken his brain with appalling grief. He banished such thoughts, almost, sometimes.

He was aware of the potential problems in utero with two fetuses. He was aware of the psychological pressures that twins would occasion. On the other hand all children had to survive in landscapes that were less than perfect, families that failed them again and again. These twins would have good parents and all would be well. He began to read the vast literature of twin studies. He had no interest in the ones that spoke of twins separated at birth liking the same brand of breakfast cereal twenty years later. He was interested in the more complex issues of how they vied for parental attention, how they developed different personalities one from the other. It turned out the experts did not agree on cause and effect. They were not able to explain why one twin flourished and the other curled into him- or herself. They were not sure which in- and out-of-womb experiences were causal and which were merely riders hitched to the preordained soul.

Ronit was beautiful as her stomach rose slightly beneath her white coat. All her patients approaching death could see the life growing within her. Were they jealous or sorrowful at the sight? Probably both, also pleased for their doctor. Perhaps it was a sign of good fortune that might spill over to them. She had lunch in the doctors' lounge with a friend whose husband was a younger colleague of her father's.

Her friend said, I'm happy for you, and seemed to mean it. I'll get the name of a good nanny for you from my nanny.

Ronit asked her friend, No more trouble? No, said her friend, the bad time passed. We survived.

I thought you would, said Ronit.

And then, because of the nature of her work, the chemicals that might be floating through the vents, she took a leave. She took long walks in the park. She went to movies in the afternoon. She took pregnancy gym classes and made two new friends, one also carrying twins.

Dr. Z. did not think the few poems the poet produced on the subject of his wife's pregnancy were among his best. He found them coy.

There was an emergency one night. Ronit called, she had a terrible pain under her navel. The obstetrician, someone she had trained with, told her to go to the emergency room. Dr. Z. and his wife dressed quickly and met her there. The poet was trembling. Don't tremble, Dr. Z. wanted to say but didn't. Ronit was swept away from them. The poet was with her. It was too soon. Dr. Z.'s wife held his hand. I'm sure it's nothing, she said with her usual disposition to ignore the beast with long teeth running right at her. I hate God, said Dr. Z. You don't believe in God, said his wife. Nevertheless, said Dr. Z., I hate Him. But no more than a half hour had passed when Ronit and the poet emerged and they were smiling. A small hernia had caused the pain. It would go away or they might operate after she delivered. It was nothing. It did not threaten the babies who were doing whatever they did in the dark of the womb, float, touch, dream. Do fetuses dream and if so do they have nightmares?

When Dr. Z. had his own children he had been very engaged in learning his trade. He went four times a week to his own analyst. He watched his son and then his daughter, checking the milestones, muscle flexibility, and eye contact. He was assured and assured his wife, they were normal children. Actually he thought they were better than normal but he knew that was vanity and pride and ego and not necessarily objective truth. He nevertheless found them extraordinary. He forgave himself that delusion: it was so common.

He was supervised twice a week by another analyst who watched his work like the tax man auditing the local mobster. He was fascinated by himself at that time. He was fascinated by his patients, but his children as they arrived in his life seemed natural, like his degrees, expected, appreciated, but hardly astonishing. He knew the medicine, had done the obstetrics rotation, had delivered four babies on his own. It was heady. He remembered a nurse wiping away tears from his eyes that were staining his mask. But after all it was only one of the amazing moments of his life.

Now, this with Ronit, this was everything. Was this about his own genes? Was his attention on these not yet breathing babies just an expression of ego, of the human desire to live on and on? Dr. Z. conceded that possibility. But maybe not. Ronit wanted these babies. She wanted to be their mother, not knowing yet how they might hurt her, how she would grow fearful for their very lives, and how her own life would never again be hers to lose or to live. His ignorant daughter wanted these babies and he wanted her, no, more than wanted, needed her, to have what she wanted. He would not be able to bear her grief if anything should happen. He had no bargaining chips to offer fate. He had no recourse if he were denied. He could only wait, a father who loved his daughter, too much maybe, but maybe when it came to love there was no such thing as too much or at least there shouldn't be.

Emotions cannot be measured like chemicals in vials. That was one thing that attracted him to psychiatry in the first place. The proper amounts were always in flux and attempts to measure the mind always failed. He liked that: that he considered real poetry.

Then as the due date approached and the heartbeats remained steady and the sonograms showed two little boys, floating about in the shadows, he found himself afraid of death: not his own, but theirs. He tried to analyze his fear, he considered his father's sudden heart attack, his mother's slow fade as arteries narrowed. He thought of Yorick and Hamlet and the alas of it all. He thought of graves and wars and outer space with its vast emptiness and none of it relieved his anxiety about Ronit and the twins who would come in their own good time, just after Ronit's fortieth birthday. The poet was composing a poem to welcome his sons. The grandfather-to-be was having stomach troubles, was it anxiety or ulcers? He would have it checked later.

And then, as he and his wife were walking down the aisle at the Metropolitan Opera House, moving slowly toward their season seats, their favorite opera, *La Traviata*, only ten minutes from curtain time, his cell phone rang. He answered it furtively. It was the poet, they were on their way to the hospital. There had been some loss of amniotic fluid. There had been some intermittent contractions. Their doctor wanted them in the hospital, a cesarean might be needed.

Dr. Z. and his wife missed that performance at the Met. It was unfortunate that they had decided to purchase the better seats for that year's subscription, seats that were now conspicuously empty in the center of the sixth row.

Dr. Z. wanted to go to the hospital. The poet had suggested they go home and he would call with word and then they could come. Dr. Z. felt he should be by his daughter's side but then remembered that he shouldn't.

He stood by the window in his living room looking at the Hudson River, black and still. He saw the lights of the looming apartment buildings on the Jersey shore, the steep cliffs beneath them, the George Washington Bridge delicately uniting the shores. He saw a small tugboat anchored halfway across, its dark shape reminding him of the Egyptian canoes that carried the dead into the underworld, stacked with the necessities of life, the memories of their breathing days. Why was he thinking about death now? The answer was obvious. The birth of the twins was the signal for his own death to approach. It marked the moment when the torch of life was passed on. It was sweet but bittersweet.

And then a freighter went slowly by. There was a light on its prow and several in the cabin. What was the long black boat, shaped like a coffin, carrying? He couldn't see. It was an omen. He didn't believe in omens. The freighter had a small red taillight that reflected in the water, ripples of neon curves in the darkness. He spent a half hour trying to decide: an omen of what?

And what of the babies? He had heard no names suggested. He wasn't concerned about their names.

He thought, because he couldn't help it, of the terrible things that might be. The diseases that the amnio couldn't identify. Of the fine wiring of the brain in which the smallest error could result in the most serious of deficits. If a neuron of a synapse drifted perhaps a hundredth of a millimeter off course, then a brain and its body could end up in an alleyway wrapped in a torn blanket on a freezing cold night or it could do harm to its mate or it could be walled into itself and suffer exile from the heat of other bodies. If a neuron strayed, if a synapse clogged and paused at the wrong second, a brain could become evil. Dr. Z. did believe in evil. Santa Claus, Elijah, werewolves, vampires, they were myths, but evil and guilt, they were as real as the bones of his body.

He named the deficits, all the ones he could think of, as if naming them would scare them away, as if naming them, staring them in the face, would spare the children, would guarantee their ordinariness. He repeated the word *autistic* four times, because he knew what that curse would mean, for child and parent. He tried to stop himself. Morbid and ridiculous, he called himself names but he couldn't stop. And then, exhausted, he went on to the less disastrous but still calamitous conditions, situations, problems that shape experience, determine happiness, competency, education, income. He thought of all the attention deficit disorders, he thought of excessive shyness, of paranoia, of uncontrolled aggressions. He thought of polars, bi, and depressions, singular. Standing there at the window he felt as if he could not breathe, as if his lungs had stalled—too much was being asked of them.

He wanted a cigarette. There were none in the house.

And then he thought of sex. He wanted sexual happiness for these little boys, not yet of course, but one day, and he knew that the genes carried those impulses forward. Genetic plans could be altered by the oddest of small matters, a connection between a serious earache and an enema could excite something best left unexcited. A desire to be the other sex could come in the genes, in the biology, or it could come in a parent's preference for a girl or a boy or in a teasing playground incident or in the air when the windows were open, like Peter Pan flying into Wendy's nursery. Sex could be thwarted, misdirected, colored with fantasies of pain inflicted or experienced. The wires in the child's brain were like radio receptors receiving commands from worlds unknown, malevolent or benevolent by whim. Whose whim? No one's whim, at any moment a man could become a cockroach.

Pollutants in the air, pollutants in the black heart of schoolteachers, nannies documented or undocumented, could shift the destiny of a child one way or another. Squalls of misery could come from a broken friendship, a failure to accomplish a task some other child could do easily. What if these children succumbed to the long litany of troubles he heard from his patients, fears, phobias, desires to harm, a sense of failure, realistic or not.

Dr. Z. stopped himself. He had become a psychoanalytic hypochondriac. He seemed to himself less like a grandparent than an analyst in desperate need of an analyst. He thought of calling Dr. H., but then the hour was late and what would he say after all? I'm worried about my grandchildren not yet born and whether or not the vicissitudes of living will destroy them.

He knew what Dr. H. would say. Those vicissitudes of yours, that's just living. Dangerous of course, but perhaps you should focus on starting a college fund for the children or imagine giving them each a microscope, or perhaps a kite with a long red tail on their tenth birthday. Have a pleasant daydream, good night. That is what Dr. H. would say. He didn't need to call him.

Dr. Z. was worrying about whether one twin would dominate the other and the possibility of a fixed unequal relationship developing between the stronger and the weaker one. He thought of Jacob and Esau and how he had always held a particular sympathy for Esau who seemed unloved by his mother.

What was wrong with being a hairy man who liked to hunt? He thought too of how he had wished his own brother ill on more than one occasion. He was getting very tired, standing there at the window. The lights in the apartment buildings on the Jersey side had mostly disappeared. Large dark shadows of buildings stood like concrete and iron vultures above the water.

Come to bed, said his wife. No, he said. I don't want to undress and then dress again. And then, as he looked out the window and returned to his melancholy musings, a sharp sound caught his attention: the phone.

Everything is fine, said the poet in a tone that aimed for calm but didn't achieve it. We named them Virgil and Isaac. Virgil is five pounds and Isaac is four and a half. They are lying under a warming lamp right now. And you can come and see them. Floor 5, room 306. Ronit is resting. She said to tell you to hurry and to please bring a hairbrush, she forgot hers.

thirteen

After a near arrest in LA Betty Gordon, a.k.a. Justine Fast, returned to New York on the red-eye and took a taxi with her rose-colored roll-on luggage to her ex-boyfriend's apartment in SoHo. He wasn't there. Wherever he was he wasn't answering her cell. The doorman wouldn't let her wait in the apartment even though she had kept her key. No girls, he had been told, none at all. She called her mother.

It had come to that.

She had dark circles under her eyes, a result of mascara that had spread like an oil spill and fatigue that had been caused by her inability to sleep without the aids she had a few weeks ago declared off limits. The flickering light within her burned sufficiently to ignite her wish to live and live on, to counter the desire to sleep forever, to want to go home and start again.

Her mother took one look at her daughter, the stale nicotine smell filled her nostrils as she pulled her child, no longer a child, into her arms and led her to her old room, which now had a couch bed, a desk for her mother's computer, and a new carpet.

Betty remembered what had happened to the old carpet. The posters were down, the lipstick messages on the mirror were gone. The room had been sanitized as if a victim of an infectious disease had died there. Betty understood. She had tried to erase herself so she couldn't blame her mother for finishing the job.

Betty took a shower and changed her clothes before her father came home from his office. Her hair was cut like a boy's. Blue, pink, crimson, yellow, purple spiked through her head: a fading firecracker, lights sinking in the moonless sky. Her father kept his eyes away from her arms. He didn't want to see what might be there. Dr. Berman might see me, she said. No, said her father. She's not well.

What? said Betty.

She's not young, said her mother.

I know, said Betty. I want to see her, she said.

You can't, said her father.

I can, said Betty.

No, said her father, you can't. But you can see Dr. H.

Dr. H. opened the door to his new patient. He showed her the coat closet. He thought about Dr. Berman. She would not have appreciated the tattoo he saw on his patient's neck when she bent down to pick up the red leather bag that she then held close to her chest while inspecting him carefully. He sat still and let her absorb his size, his blue shirt, the glasses that slipped a little to the left, the receding hairline, the jagged scar on his left hand where he had cut himself while carving the Thanksgiving turkey.

You're ordinary, she said.

Is ordinary so bad? he asked.

Yes, she said.

Tell me why, he said.

He looked at her and smiled. It was a shy smile but it cast a glow into the consulting room. He saw the pieces of her flying around in her head. He saw the little girl waking from a night terror and screaming for her mother. He saw the fragile glass of her soul, tipping back and forth, ready to fall, and he saw the colors of her hair, brave sparks. She was still there.

I want to be special, she said.

You are special, he said. Everyone is.

She sighed.

Blah, blah, blah, she said.

What do you hope for? he asked.

And Betty couldn't answer because she hoped for so much at once and she had little hope.

Dr. H. waited.

I want to see Dr. Berman, she said.

Let's try, he said, you and me, and see if we can work together.

I don't need a shrink, she said to her father, knowing the word irritated him. I need a God with many arms.

Try the Asia Society gift shop, said her father.

Betty's agent called her. There's a part for you in the new Coen brothers script. You wanna try for it? They called and asked for you.

No, she said. Not now.

It wasn't that she didn't like it when the cameras were on her face. She liked it. It wasn't that she didn't want people to know her name. She did. It was just that she wanted to stay home now. She didn't want her name in the tabloids. What did she want? How should she know?

What do I want? she asked Dr. H.

You tell me, he said.

She rose from her chair, glared at him. Useless, she said, you are useless.

But two days later she was there at the appointed hour. Dr. H. was not surprised.

Betty met her old high school friend in a wine bar and amid the dark bottles, the cheese plates, the noise, the rising drumbeat of trysts and tales of betrayal, movies liked or not, raises denied or won, romances budding or fading, she spoke of her old boyfriend. Had she really loved him? Had she ever really loved anyone? How do you know if you love someone? she asked her friend. You know, said her friend. Betty sipped at her fake beer. Stop feeling sorry for yourself, she thought. Stop being such a baby. The word *stop* rolled around again and again in her brain. I could stop everything if I wanted to, she said to herself. Do I want to?

Two tables over someone recognized Betty. That's Justine Fast. Heads turned, staring. I'm surprised she's not in prison, a loud voice offered. Betty turned her head to the left. She wanted them to see her best side, the one that photographed perfectly. She felt ashamed and she felt excited. She was someone. Wasn't she someone? It was good to be someone. It was not good to be someone. Betty's friend's cell phone rang. She turned her back to Betty and in order to block the noise from the bar put her other hand over her ear. She slipped down from her high stool and stood against the wall, her back to the room. Betty put her hand in the backpack that had been left on the floor. In an instant she had zipped open the small pocket, fished out a wallet, emptied its contents into her own lap, and replaced the wallet.

Betty's friend had to go. Her sister was waiting uptown.

Alone in the bar, Betty fondled the dollars in her lap. Am I a thief? she wondered. Would she report this act to Dr. H.? Would he be shocked? He was not allowed to be shocked. It would be unprofessional of him to be shocked. It would be a joy to shock him. Would he admire her daring? Maybe.

Dr. H. asked Betty, Were you angry at your friend?

No, I just thought it would be cool to defund her.

Did you think she had something else you wanted? Dr. H. leaned forward in his chair. There was no note of accusation in his tone. On the other hand, no admiration either.

Maybe, said Betty.

What? he asked.

It's exciting to take things, said Betty.

I imagine so, said Dr. H., rising to indicate their time was up.

Paxil, Zoloft, the right amount of which was hard to determine: Dr. H. wrote the Rx, but only for a few at a time. Betty was given by her aunt a not very frequently used gym membership. She endured a long, very boring test to see if attention deficit disorder contributed to her jangled nerves. She told her periodontist that she didn't want to be Justine anymore but wasn't fond of Betty either. If it was attention deficit disorder they would use Ritalin. It wasn't. Sometimes she slept too long into the late morning. Sometimes she couldn't sleep at all. A psychologist administered an IQ test. Betty didn't want to take the test. She gave wild answers or no answers. The results were not useful.

A lost lamb, said her mother.

A not so adorable wolf, said her father.

What did we do wrong? asked her mother for the ten thousandth time.

I'm not talking about this anymore said her father, although he would, in bed, at dinner, after the movies, on a walk in the park.

She was good in front of the camera, said her mother.

So was Lassie, said her father.

The months passed. She mostly made her appointments.

The world is corrupt, she said. Every politician lies. No one cares about you if you're poor and if you try to be someone a crazy person will kill you. Jodie Foster was almost murdered. John Lennon is dead.

Woody Allen lives, said Dr. H.

I'd like to get him in bed, said Betty.

He'd like that, thought Dr. H., but waited for her to continue.

As she sat across from him he smelled her perfume, applied like insect repellent in black fly season. She wasn't kind. She had a guilty conscience, a superego that plagued her, but she knew how to keep her self-criticism from changing her plans. She rejected his interpretations. She wore skirts so short he had to focus his eyes on the seventeenth century print of an Italian landscape he had purchased in Florence years ago that hung just above her head.

However, Dr. H. was a patient man. He and the Paxil would win in the end. It was just a matter of time. Did he have the time before something happened, an overdose, a major theft that landed her in prison, a drunken evening that would end in a car crash, in a drowning in a swimming pool, a fall from a tree she had climbed so she could be above everyone else. If she had plans for ending her life she did not tell him. Sometimes she stayed home and sulked in her bedroom, watching TV until the stations went off the air and then opening her iPod and downloading streaming rap music until dawn. At least that kind of evening would lead to morning, so thought Dr. H.

Was she taking drugs other than the ones he was prescribing for her? Dr. H. thought not. He wanted to think not. Sometimes when she was in his office he felt her presence as if a small bird were flying about the room, its heart beating in terror, its wings frayed, its beak pecking wildly at anything in its way, its small feet clinging to shelf, to book, to clock, to arm of the chair, to the box of crayons he kept for children, to doorknob, a stray feather falling here and there, a cold-eyed canary bird moving and moving so you could not hold it in your hands, so you could not bring it in close to your chest, so you could not let your breath flow onto its back and soothe that flipping, frightened heart.

And once in a while she would come in and sit quietly in the chair and say nothing for a long while and he would wonder if she was sleeping even though her eyes were open. He would wonder if she had taken too many or too few of his prescriptions. He would wonder if she was still there and would come back before the end of the session. When that happened he felt as if she were trying to punish him. But maybe he was judging himself, found himself wanting, was impatient with his own skills, and maybe she knew that and worried about his lack of faith in her, in himself. He really hated the sessions that were filled with this awful quiet no words of his could alter.

Betty, you could go back to school, said her mother.

Call your agent, said her father.

I don't want to act, she said.

But that is all you wanted to do for years, said her mother.

It's what you wanted me to do, said Betty.

It is not. I didn't care, said her mother. You were always dressing up, pretending to be this or that. You loved the music videos. You wanted voice lessons and acting lessons. I wanted you to be a doctor. I wanted you to pass algebra.

You need a face-lift, Betty said to her mother. Your chins are sagging. Her mother left the room.

At her next appointment with Dr. H. she reported the scene to Dr. H. She began to sing, *On top of Old Smokey I lost my true love.* He asked her if her mother was her true love? Her, never, said Betty. Your father? he offered. That remark was followed by a long silence, a silence that lasted until the end of the session.

One Thursday, she said, I might join the army.

Christ, Dr. H. thought, and bit his inner cheek. Tell me what that might be like, he said.

One Tuesday she came to her session in a low-cut silk dress and pearls around her neck. Was it a double strand? She seemed to have come to life from the cover of a fashion magazine, the one Dr. H. kept on a side table in his waiting room, except for the fact that all the colors of the rainbow still ran through her hair as if she were a child's toy in the window of a cut-rate drugstore. The effect was to combine Andy Warhol with Princess Diana.

Do you like my pearls? she asked as she sat down.

Did you pay for them? he asked.

Guess? she said to him.

Did you pay for them? he asked again.

She wasn't going to answer him, which was its own answer.

He knew the diagnosis. This *borderline* word that brought to mind smugglers and desperate immigrants, but actually referred to the wall between reason and unreason: boiling thoughts that had lost their manners. This line served as the barrier to unseemly excitement, terrible rage, calamitous shards of the soul crossing the border, invading the daylight, denting the ego, leaving graffiti to bleed across the superego, screaming through the halls of the self.

But the diagnosis, the cold words in the manual, they could not begin to describe the thing in Betty, the things in Betty, that tormented her. It was as if a thousand roaches invaded the kitchen night after night, and no poison spray would stop them, no rank odor prevent their arrival, no stepping on them or sweeping them up in the best of Dyson vacuums. They came, these roaches of the mind, through the cracks, through the tiles on the floor, out of the cabinets, everywhere roaches sneak and hide. And when he saw Betty that way Dr. H. felt anger, not at Betty, but at the illness he intended to vanquish. He knew the mighty strength of his enemy, and he saw clearly the fragile hold on life held by his patient, the one with the smile he found himself increasingly eager to evoke, anxious to encourage. Careful, he said to himself, very careful.

Betty hung up on her agent when he called again to press her to audition for a new TV series. Betty went to the park and sat on a bench in the playground. She watched the up and down and in and out of the climbing rails. She saw the children hanging by their hands from bars, slipping down the slide, crossing small bridges, swinging on a tire held by a chain to the entire contraption. She watched carefully the faces of the children. She was checking for fear. Sometimes she saw it. Just before the push-off, the reach of a hand to a bar, just before the foot leans into a higher step, fear flushes across the child's face. Betty felt sad sitting there. Do I want children one day? she asked herself. Yes, every hormone, every cell, nucleus, acid, protein, said to her. No, she said to herself, any child of mine would just be like me.

She told Dr. H. about her visit to the playground. She told him that she had sat on the edge of the sandbox and taken off her pearls and buried them a few inches down in the sand that was not like beach sand but like the crumble of gravestones. And what did you hope would happen to the pearls? asked Dr. H.

A little girl would find them and her mother would let her take them home and use them for dress-up.

Anything else about the little girl? asked Dr. H.

No, said Betty.

What might happen? asked Dr. H.

The little girl dies of leukemia and her divorced mother buries her with the pearls she used to wear when she played at being a princess.

Not such a happy story, said Dr. H.

No, agreed Betty.

Which is how the subject of death entered the consulting room.

Some months later, as Dr. H. was gently reminding his patient that most young women her age were preparing for a profession, to do something in the real world, and she was reminding him that she had already earned enough money to live for years and years and she wasn't interested in money anyway. He said, Let's pretend you needed to do something, what would it be?

She knew. She knew exactly. I would write books for children. I would write good books for children.

He said, I wouldn't stop you.

Something is stopping me, she said, and began to cry. Makeup ran, blotches came, she caught tears on her tongue. She began to have trouble breathing. The session was over. At the door she turned around and said, I feel dizzy. Dr. H. knew she was an actress and could faint whenever she wanted. He would rather she didn't: not in his office. He would really rather she didn't.

And so of course there was a new boyfriend. Gregg was a cameraman with one of the national news shows. They met in a club. They screamed out their names to one another as the lights circled around. They danced a war dance or was it a love dance for several hours before they exchanged names. He knew who she was or had been. He was impressed but not cowed. She liked his face. He was political. She was pre-political. She intended to have more opinions one day. He lived in Washington Heights in an apartment with a view of the river and the rocky cliffs on the Jersey side. He had grown up in Maine and he had a stern, weathered look, a young man who couldn't be melted down or blown apart and he had no drug history. He drank only moderately and he, best of all, had no girlfriend, the last one having left him for her boss, receiving a far better job as a reward. He had no weird sexual habits and if his fantasies were dark he didn't share them with her. Betty gained a few pounds and was trying to quit smoking. He didn't like the trace of smoke that stuck to her body, remained in her ears, in her armpits, in the folds of her clothes.

I'll move in with him, she said to her mother. You just met him, her mother said. Wait at least a few months. Why? said Betty. She left the room as her mother was listing the reasons, the wisdom, the necessity of caution. I'll move in with him, she said to Dr. H., who said, How will you feel if it doesn't work out? Like hell, she said. But she'd been there before and wasn't afraid.

He liked classic movies, *Casablanca, The Third Man, The Orient Express*, Hitchcock, the Marx Brothers. They watched them late at night in his bed. Sometimes he called her Justine. She let him although she preferred Betty. During the day when he was at work Betty went to the gym and she went to see Dr. H. and she went shopping with her mother and she told her agent that she was dropping him in favor of a real life. Good luck, sweetie, he had said, and don't call if you change your mind. But then Gregg was sent out of town with a show. He would be gone for a few months. She could fly out and visit him, he said. He would be in Cambodia for a look at the death camps there. I don't think so, she said. It wasn't the airplane that frightened her. It wasn't the death camps, which he explained to her were no longer operating. It was something else.

What? asked Dr. H.

I don't know, said Betty.

And now in the week before he was to leave she turned her face away from him. She was supposed to meet him for dinner at their favorite Indian restaurant near his studio at six o'clock and she never showed up.

She had gone home again. Her mother rushed to bring her an ashtray as she curled up on the couch in her old room. Her face was not clean and her black fishnet stockings were ripped in a revealing place. Is there any rice pudding in the house? she asked her mother. Her mother went into the kitchen to make some. Gregg called. Betty wouldn't answer the phone or respond to the texts. Damn, said her father, Damn, Damn, Damn.

Dr. H. tried. Did you like *Charlotte's Web*? he asked.

Everyone likes *Charlotte's Web*, she said. Did you like *Curious George*, the mischievous monkey? he asked. Not particularly, she said. What then? he asked. *Where the Wild Things Are*, she said. You wanted to be Max? He was headed somewhere sexual. She saw him coming. No, she said. I wanted to be a wild thing. He waited. I am a wild thing, she said. In the end, he said, Max goes home. I am home, she said. I want to leave home, she added. Good, said Dr. H., who felt like stomping around his office and waving his arms and growling his growl.

Betty bought a blank notebook. She bought some watercolors. She brought them home and stored them on the top shelf of her closet under her press photos. Those she had buried under her sneakers, old sneakers she had meant to throw out but hadn't. Everything in her closet that wasn't on a hanger was on the floor. Everything was crumpled and wrinkled and she waited for her mother to straighten it out. Her mother was waiting for her to grow up. It was an impasse. It forced Betty to buy new clothes that were never right, never exactly right.

Tell me about acting, asked Dr. H.

What? she said.

Do you miss it? he asked.

No, she said.

It made me nervous, she said.

How so? he asked.

She told him.

She received a long letter from Gregg. He wished she were with him. He didn't want anything to happen to her. He had bought her a present in Phnom Penh. He asked her to be careful. He told her that he didn't want her to steal. He didn't want her to see her face in the tabloids. He was making good money on this job. He would buy her what she wanted. He thought he could spend his life taking care of her.

I don't need taking care of, she said to Dr. H.

Of course not, thought Dr. H.

What was wrong with Gregg? wondered Dr. H. Gregg wasn't his concern.

There was a bad night. It started at a club. The thug at the door hadn't recognized her. The friends she was with had to vouch for her. She had worn a lace top and it ripped as she was dancing and then she had a few drinks. She was vague on the number. Then this tall woman in black leather boots pushed her when she was already off balance with a glass in her hand and she fell to the floor and the glass broke and she went for the woman and bit her on the neck. Yes, there was a small trickle of blood, but she hadn't killed her or anything. And then she was thrown out of the club and her friends didn't come with her and so she was alone on a street that seemed empty and so she screamed some obscenity and then she went looking for a cab and she couldn't find one and so she walked and she saw what she thought was a monster coming toward her, only it was just a trash can that had been tipped by the wind.

She slept through her next appointment with Dr. H. She slept through her yoga class. Her mother heard her in the bathroom and the sounds were not pleasant.

I need a higher dose, she said to him.

I don't think so, he said.

You can manage, he added.

I can? she asked.

You can, he said.

As she left he noticed a streak of purple dye and another one of pink running down the back of her neck and disappearing under her T-shirt. For a second he thought it was blood, blood from the brain. Oozing, she's oozing out of herself, he thought, and then wrote a far more technical, professional sentence in his notebook.

Some months later, after a short vacation in which he went to Belize with his family, he heard a message on his answering machine.

Hi, it's Betty, I'm going to Cambodia, back in a few weeks, will call.

Good news or bad news, he wasn't sure.

Gregg met her in the airport. He was tan and seemed taller than she had remembered. He was shy as he grasped her arm. He lost his shyness later in his hotel room. I caught you, he said, I caught you. What did he mean? Was she some kind of lizard scurrying along the tile floor that he had trapped in an upside-down wastebasket? Did she like being caught or didn't she?

The shoot was over the next week. She went with Gregg on a riverboat ride. It would have been romantic but she didn't like the rocking motion of the boat and closed her eyes and lay down on a cushion and moaned for the whole four hours. It occurred to her that she had a gift for missing the moment.

She did not steal anything in Cambodia. Not quite true. She took a towel from the hotel. Everyone takes towels from hotels. She took a set of ten postcards from the gift shop only because the girl behind the counter was rude. She took a blue bracelet from a vendor's cart because the vendor had fallen asleep on a nearby bench and she didn't want to wake him. But she took nothing that needed to be declared on return. She was pleased.

She seems calmer since she came back from Cambodia, said her mother to her father as they waited for the water to boil for their pasta.

Remember, said her father, she can tack pretty well in a storm. This was a metaphor. She had never gone sailing with him although he had asked her several times.

Her mother said, I should have divorced you years ago. And then a minute later she added, I don't mean that.

I know you don't, he said.

I just wish—, he added.

Me too, she said.

The seasons changed and changed again. Hardly anyone recognized Betty as Justine anymore. It was all right with her. Justine Fast had died a grizzly death tied to a cactus in an imaginary desert, ants had eaten out her eyes and crawled across her skin. Minutes before the end of a session she had described this in full detail to Dr. H., who intended to return to the subject as soon as possible.

Gregg wanted to buy Betty a ring but he knew she could steal a better one and that made it hard for him to actually choose one. He finally did. Betty began a children's story, Once upon a time there was a little girl named Justine. She lived in a castle under the sea. Justine was a girl octopus and she was going to lead the battle of the octopi against the sharks that swam in the nearby reef, consuming baby octopi by the dozens. She was going to do the illustrations. It would be an epic battle. Her name would be on the cover, Betty Gordon.

Dr. Z. and Dr. H. had been to a meeting of the institute's education committee. One of their faculty had been boring his students so badly that half of them neglected to show up for class. His evaluations by the students were filled with vague phrases of neutral disinterest. They were cautious students even in anonymous evaluations. You never know whom you might need in your professional life. These students were not the sort to demonstrate on the steps of the capital or burn flags of any nation in a public place. Their chemistry experiments never exploded. Their college essays revealed only what they wanted revealed. Nevertheless they were clearly intolerably bored, which in a class on Sexual Fantasy and Its Role in the Doctor-Patient Relationship seemed unnecessary.

He has to go, said Dr. Z.

Dr. H. sighed. He didn't want to be the one to do it.

We could give him another semester, he suggested.

We could not, Dr. Z. said. What is happening with your movie star?

Her hair is all one color, said Dr. H.

That's good, said Dr. Z.

Yes, said Dr. H., and it's green.

Green? said Dr. Z.

Yes, said Dr. H., the color of spring.

fourteen

The wealthy patron beamed at the doctors at his table. It was a front table right near the podium. He had sponsored the $40,000 Dr. Estelle Berman Prize for original work. This year it was going to the author of the paper titled "On Countertransference in the Vulnerable Analyst." He was ready to push back his chair and rise to his feet, walk up the few steps to the stage and present the prize to the winner, a very young analyst.

Later that night, as the young analyst puts on his glasses so he can undo the clasp on his wife's necklace, he whispers into her ear, hurry up, and she disappears into the bathroom. As he waits he thinks of all the urges, dark and ordinary, the moods, bleak and blissful, innocent and guilty, unspoken thoughts: anxious, brave, terrified, that were even at that moment rising in the air, uniting all the apartments, crossing the park, moving uptown and downtown, punishing or rewarding minds of all economic and social varieties, moving like a mist over the high towers, the steel bridges, their cables shifting in the wind, fog covering the

Empire State, the Chrysler Building, the new Freedom Tower above its mourning pool. He thinks of all the minor resentments, the failures to love or be loved that like so many allergens in the spring float through the cross streets, the tunnels, Chinatown and Washington Heights, causing many to stay indoors. He thinks of the great battles of conscience and desire that leave scars on minds as they pause at street corners, or stand in an elevator, or are on their way to the dentist or the mammogram, or the waiting analyst.

His wife calls out from the bathroom: We're out of toilet paper.

In Central Park, across the street from where Dr. Berman had lived, the almost nineteenth-century lamps send long shadows along the paths by the deserted benches. Along the avenue an occasional bus lumbers by. In front of the Museum of Natural History the stone bodies of the stately lions are unmoved by the passing hours, the coming of the next day. All through the night dreams drift away, carrying images of fright and love, of a gentle touch or a ferocious bite, a harmless wish, a slamming and crashing and bumbling about of old angers and new ones, mingled together, forgotten by morning.

about the author

◆◆ Writer, essayist, and journalist ANNE ROIPHE is known
◆◆ and revered for such novels as *Up the Sandbox* and
Lovingkindness, and for her memoirs: *1185 Park Avenue*, *Epilogue*,
and *Art and Madness*. In addition to her eighteen fiction and
nonfiction books, she has written articles for *The New York
Times Magazine*, *Vogue*, and *Elle*, among others, and for many
years she wrote columns for *The New York Observer* and for *The
Jerusalem Report*. Her book, *Fruitful*, was a finalist for the National
Book Award.

about seven stories press

Seven Stories Press is an independent book publisher based in New York City. We publish works of the imagination by such writers as Nelson Algren, Russell Banks, Octavia E. Butler, Ani DiFranco, Assia Djebar, Ariel Dorfman, Coco Fusco, Barry Gifford, Martha Long, Luis Negrón, Hwang Sok-yong, Lee Stringer, and Kurt Vonnegut, to name a few, together with political titles by voices of conscience, including Subhankar Banerjee, the Boston Women's Health Collective, Noam Chomsky, Angela Y. Davis, Human Rights Watch, Derrick Jensen, Ralph Nader, Loretta Napoleoni, Gary Null, Greg Palast, Project Censored, Barbara Seaman, Alice Walker, Gary Webb, and Howard Zinn, among many others. Seven Stories Press believes publishers have a special responsibility to defend free speech and human rights, and to celebrate the gifts of the human imagination, wherever we can. In 2012 we launched Triangle Square books for young readers with strong social justice and narrative components, telling personal stories of courage and commitment. For additional information, visit www.sevenstories.com.